D0006839

CLASS PETS

Fuzzy Takes Charge

CLASS PETS

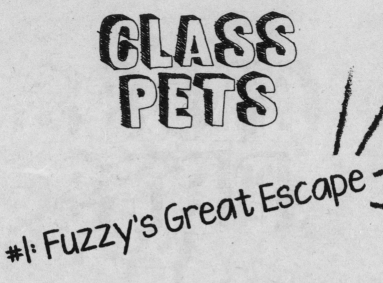

#1: Fuzzy's Great Escape

#2: Fuzzy Takes Charge

#3: Fuzzy Freaks Out

#4: Fuzzy Fights Back

CLASS PETS

#2: Fuzzy Takes Charge

Bruce Hale

Scholastic Inc.

Text and illustrations copyright © 2018 by Bruce Hale

This book is being published simultaneously in hardcover by Scholastic Press.

All rights reserved. Published by Scholastic Inc., *Publishers since 1920.* SCHOLASTIC, SCHOLASTIC PRESS, and associated logos are trademarks and/or registered trademarks of Scholastic Inc.

The publisher does not have any control over and does not assume any responsibility for author or third-party websites or their content.

This book is a work of fiction. Names, characters, places, and incidents are either the product of the author's imagination or are used fictitiously, and any resemblance to actual persons, living or dead, business establishments, events, or locales is entirely coincidental.

ISBN 978-1-338-14521-2

10 9 8 7 6 5 4 3 2   18 19 20 21 22

Printed in the U.S.A.   40

First printing 2018

Book design by Baily Crawford

To Laura Ginoza and all the
cool keikis at Pearl City
Elementary

CONTENTS

Chapter 1: Stranger Danger 1

Chapter 2: What Do You Do with a Dud Sub? 11

Chapter 3: Send In the Splash Squad 27

Chapter 4: Operation Wet Robot 39

Chapter 5: Piggy Prison 47

Chapter 6: Flake Out 55

Chapter 7: Hide and Go "Eek!" 71

Chapter 8: Rock the Note 81

Chapter 9: Stowaway Piggy 93

Chapter 10: Fuzzy the Spy 103

Chapter 11: A Bobo No-No 111

Chapter 12: Fuzzy Takes Flight 121

Chapter 13: Idol Threats 129

Chapter 14: The "Ick" Factor 141

Chapter 15: Brittle Go Peep 151

Chapter 16: Cloudy with a Dance of Meatballs 161

Chapter 17: A Whiter Shade of Fail 173

CHAPTER 1

Stranger Danger

It was a Monday mystery. When Fuzzy returned to Room 5-B after a weekend with student-of-the-week Maya, he just knew that something was wrong. True, his sniffer was still in shock from the tropical mango shampoo Maya had used on him that morning.

Even so, Fuzzy smelled danger.

As Maya gently lifted him from the pet carrier into his cage, his senses went on high alert. Fuzzy scampered over the pine shavings to check out his home. Had someone kidnapped his favorite blue ball? Nope. There it was in the corner, same as he'd left it.

Was a hungry cat stalking through the classroom? Fuzzy rose onto his hind legs and did a quick scan. Nothing but sleepy fifth graders preparing for their lessons, same as usual.

Sitting back down, he scratched himself. Could he have been imagining things? It was true, Fuzzy had a terrific imagination. That was, after all, what had won him his post as the Class Pets Club's director of adventure. (Well, that and his sense of adventure.)

But the prickly feeling down his spine wasn't mange mites, and it wouldn't go away. Closing his eyes, Fuzzy took a deep, deep whiff. Beyond the usual odors of freshly sharpened pencils, chalk dust, and peanut butter sandwiches lurked an odd new smell.

A stranger.

And just then, Fuzzy realized that a familiar scent was missing: the sweet, fresh-baked bread aroma of Miss Wills, Room 5-B's teacher. His eyes popped open, searching for her.

She was nowhere to be seen. Instead, a man stood by Miss Wills's desk with his arms crossed. Scowling, he surveyed the room.

"Holy haystacks!" chirped Fuzzy.

Of medium height for a human, the man was stiffer than a stale breadstick and just as skinny. His close-cropped hair was dull brown, his clothes were the color of mud, and he looked like he'd been sucking on a lemon so long, the pucker had stuck.

"Who the heck is that?" Fuzzy wondered.

The bell rang. The mysterious man glared at the students until their conversations faltered and died off. Waiting until the room was completely silent, he then cleared his throat.

"My name," he said in a tight tenor voice, "is . . ."

Gripping a piece of chalk, he pivoted and scratched his name onto the board with a grating squeak.

"Mr. Brittle," the stiff man concluded. He whipped back around, eyeing the fifth graders as if they'd tried to steal his wallet while his back was turned. "And I do not tolerate any nonsense in my classroom."

His classroom? The students traded puzzled looks.

Fuzzy frowned. Where was Miss Wills? Had this stranger done something to her? His hackles rose. Fuzzy considered himself a guinea pig of peace, but if the situation demanded, he could bite with the best of them.

Loud Brandon raised his hand. It stayed up for a long time as Mr. Brittle finished giving everyone the evil eye. Finally, the stiff man nodded, granting permission for the student to speak.

"Where's Miss Wills?" asked Brandon.

"In court," said Mr. Brittle.

Several kids gasped. Fuzzy cocked his head. He'd heard of basketball courts and tennis courts, but he had no idea why Miss Wills would be playing sports instead of teaching class.

"Is she being sued?" Zoey-with-the-braces burst out.

Mr. Brittle snapped, "Children who wish to speak in my class raise their hands first."

Zoey rolled her eyes, but she lifted her hand as directed. The man pointed a finger at her.

4

"Is Miss Wills being sued?" she repeated.

"Certainly not."

"Then, why—?"

"Miss Wills has been called in for jury duty."

Maya's forehead crinkled. "What's that?" At the teacher's meaningful glare, she hoisted her arm into the air and repeated the question.

Scanning the room, Mr. Brittle asked, "Does anyone know the answer?"

The students shrugged. Raising his hand, Loud Brandon asked, "Is jury duty what happens when a jury has to go to the bathroom?"

A few kids giggled, until the teacher's scowl shut them up.

"Wrong *and* rude," said the man. "Anyone else? No? Not a very bright bunch, are we, *hmm*?"

Fuzzy's eyes widened. How mean! Miss Wills would never speak to her class like that.

"Jury duty is when citizens serve on the jury for a trial," said Mr. Brittle. "Your teacher will be gone all week, maybe longer. I am her substitute."

Miss Wills, gone?

"No!" squeaked Fuzzy. "No, no, no!"

The substitute's close-cropped head swiveled in his direction like a tank turret zeroing in on a target. "And what," he said, "is *that*?"

Once more, he ignored the students' answers until they had raised their hands. Finally, he called on Spiky Diego, one of Fuzzy's favorites.

"Fuzzy is a guinea pig," said the boy.

Mr. Brittle's eyes narrowed. "I am not as dim as you are. I *know* what a guinea pig looks like. I want to know *why* that pig is in my classroom."

Fuzzy bristled. "I'm no pig—I'm a rodent!"

"Noisy little thing," the teacher sneered.

"He's our class pet," said Diego. "Kind of a mascot."

The substitute's nostrils twitched as if he'd smelled something funky. "They carry disease. They are the same filthy creatures that caused the bubonic plague."

"Wasn't that rats?" asked Maya, ever the history buff.

"Same difference," said Mr. Brittle.

Connor lifted his hand. "Actually, I think it was the *fleas* on the rats that—"

Whap! The substitute thwacked a ruler onto the desktop. The kids jumped, startled.

"If I want history, I will watch PBS!" he said. "That pig is a distraction, and I want it gone."

An *oooh!* swelled in the classroom. Nearly everyone's hands shot up.

"Yes, the fat boy." Mr. Brittle pointed his ruler at Heavy-Handed Jake.

Fuzzy gaped. Nobody in 5-B talked like that. This man had already broken the classroom's no-bullying policy, and he hadn't even been around for fifteen minutes!

Jake blushed furiously. "Um, Fuzzy is Miss Wills's personal pet. I don't think she'd like you getting rid of him."

The substitute's knuckles tightened around the ruler. He glowered at Jake for a moment, then turned and stalked up to Fuzzy's cage. Wielding the straight-edge like a sword, Mr. Brittle growled, "You had better mind your manners, mister. I hear that in Peru, they *eat* guinea pigs."

Suffering mange mites! Shocked to the core, Fuzzy shrank behind his igloo. He heard students gasp.

Mr. Brittle wheeled on the class. "Enough time-wasting. We will begin our lessons, and I warn you"—again, he brandished the ruler—"you had better not try any tricks with me, you little snots. Because I. Hate. Tricks." On each of his last three words, the sub smacked the straightedge on Fuzzy's table. *Whack-whack-whack!*

Nerves frazzled, Fuzzy huddled behind one of his blocks and watched the substitute sneer and bully his way through the morning. One whole week of this? Fuzzy didn't think he could stand it. More important, he didn't think his students could stand it.

Somebody had to do something. The kids were powerless, so that meant *he* had to do something.

But what?

Fuzzy didn't know. Still, as he brooded, gnawing on the corner of his block, one thing became crystal clear.

Whatever the method, whatever it took, this sub must go.

CHAPTER 2

What Do You Do with a Dud Sub?

Some things you just have to see to believe. Miss Wills always told her students that when people first heard of the giraffe, they laughed and thought it was a myth. Likewise, Fuzzy wouldn't have believed Mr. Brittle if he hadn't seen him with his own eyes.

The sub didn't crack jokes. He didn't laugh. He didn't eat. He didn't drink. He just droned on and on in that flat, tight voice, like some kind of lean, mean teaching machine. (With emphasis on the *mean*.)

By the end of the day, the man had wilted Spiky Diego's hair with his insults, made the whole front row jumpy, and brought Nervous Lily to tears. The fifth graders who left the room after the last bell seemed completely different from the kids who'd entered that morning. They slunk out like beaten dogs: downcast, dispirited, and depressed.

Watching this pitiful parade, Fuzzy growled deep in his throat. He focused all his attention on the enemy, searching for weaknesses.

Fuzzy noticed that Mr. Brittle's rigid behavior didn't change when the students had gone. He lined up all his papers just so, stowing them meticulously in his messenger bag. He aligned his pens to be perfectly parallel with the desk's edge.

When the sub glanced up and caught Fuzzy observing him, he stalked over to the cage. "Three words for you, hairball: piggy pot pie."

"You wouldn't dare!" chirped Fuzzy, acting tougher than he felt. He knew the man couldn't understand him, but he had to say something.

Whack! Whack! Whack! Whack! In a flash, Mr. Brittle whipped out his ruler and smacked it on the cage.

Wheek! Fuzzy jumped straight up and scurried to hide in his igloo. All this whacking played havoc with his nerves. Someone should steal that man's ruler.

The sub snorted. Collecting his messenger bag and jacket, he marched out the door as stiffly as if someone had starched his shorts. The lock turned. Then, *tok tok tok*, his hard heels clicked down the hallway, steady as a metronome.

Fuzzy blew out a sigh. He had met a fair number of people for your average rodent, but he'd never met anyone like Mr. Brittle. How could any human be so, so . . . inhuman? Maybe the other pets knew something about the man. Maybe he'd substituted for one of their teachers before. Fuzzy couldn't wait to ask them.

But, of course, he had to wait.

Fifteen minutes later, the door opened again, this time admitting Darius Poole, Leo Gumpus

Elementary's ace custodian. A smiling beanpole in tan coveralls, Mr. Darius enjoyed rockstar status with the students, and he sure knew how to treat a pet. Week in, week out, the pockets of his jumpsuit produced an astonishing array of grapes, carrots, and other tasty treats.

"Hey, little buddy," he greeted Fuzzy as he strolled over to the cage. "Another perfect day in paradise?"

"Not really," said Fuzzy.

His expression must have said it all, because the custodian reached into the open-topped cage and picked him up for a snuggle. The big man wasn't as cuddly, or as sweet smelling, as Miss Wills. (Her fresh-baked bread aroma beat his sweat and lemony cleansers anytime.) Still, Fuzzy found that the cuddling calmed him.

"Aw, you miss your teacher?" said Mr. Darius.

"You have no idea," said Fuzzy.

The custodian stroked him, slipping him a wilted parsley sprig from his pocket. "Sorry about the soggy greens, amigo. Lunch leftovers."

Fuzzy accepted his treat without complaint—hey, even droopy parsley is still parsley—and the custodian returned him to his cage. With calm efficiency, Mr. Darius swept the room, emptied the wastebaskets, and cleaned the chalkboard. Then, with a cheery "Later, dude," he was gone.

As soon as the door clicked shut, Fuzzy sprang into action. First, he shoved his plastic platform up against the cage wall. Then he nosed his ball over beside it and braced the ball with two wooden blocks.

When he was certain that all was secure, he scrambled up, up, up—from block to ball to platform—and over the cage wall. *Whoomf!* Fuzzy landed, a little breathless, on the table that held his home.

He smiled to himself. Maybe guinea pigs weren't the world's best climbers, but thanks to the advice of his old friend Geronimo the rat, Fuzzy could stage a breakout with the best of them.

As he made his way across the room and up the cubbyholes, Fuzzy couldn't help but recall Geronimo,

Room 6-C's pet. The old rat had retired last summer to a farm, and Fuzzy missed his craftiness. Geronimo could have evicted an evil substitute in no time flat. Fuzzy hoped that he and the other class pets could match the rat's cunning.

After scaling the bookshelf to the very top, Fuzzy stood on tiptoe and shoved aside a loose ceiling tile. Then, with a heave-ho and an *oof*, he pulled himself up into the crawl space. There, he paused to catch his breath. One of these days, he was going to have to do more pull-ups and push-ups. One of these days, he was going to really get in shape.

But not today.

Bristling with purpose, Fuzzy trotted along between the ducts, pipes, and struts that cluttered the drop ceiling, trying to ignore its slightly spooky vibe. He was headed for the forgotten nook above Room 2-B's closet that had become the Class Pets' clubhouse.

Geronimo had started their club so the pets

would have something to do after hours, but it had become so much more than that. It was a support group, a gossip clearinghouse, and, ever since Fuzzy had led them on a field trip, an adventure club.

Fuzzy clasped his paws as he peered down into the clubhouse. He felt his heart lift. By the light of some borrowed votive candles, the other six pets sprawled about their cozy, pillow-strewn hideaway, chatting and catching up with one another. Fuzzy scampered down the ramp to join them.

Yes, he'd had a tough day. Yes, he faced a challenging situation, but he was sure that his fellow pets would have his back. After all, they were a resourceful, serious-minded bunch.

"Brother Fuzzy!" Cinnabun, the flop-eared bunny, greeted him. "Bless your heart, you're just in time to sing the club song with us."

Fuzzy skidded to a halt at the foot of the ramp. "Not now," he said. "There's an important—"

"Pish-posh," said Cinnabun. "As club president, I do declare that there's nothing more important at this moment than singing our theme song."

"But—" Fuzzy began.

"Are all of y'all ready?" asked the bunny. "Then we'll begin. A-one, two, three, and . . ."

In several different keys, the pets belted out:

"Ohhh, a classroom pet is loyal
And faithful through and through
We'll snuggle when you're happy
We'll cheer you when you're blue
To help our kids and teachers,
There's nothing we won't do
Hey, riddle-dee-dee and riddle-dee-dum
A class pet's always true!"

About halfway through, Fuzzy gave up trying to interrupt and joined in. Once Cinnabun got started on a song, there was no stopping her. After a final couple rounds of riddle-dee-dums, the music finally lurched to a halt, and Fuzzy was able to get a word in.

"You've got to help me," he said. "There's big trouble."

"Fiddle-faddle," said Cinnabun. "Everyone knows that singing scares your troubles away."

"Not this time," said Fuzzy.

"What's wrong?" asked Mistletoe the mouse. Her whiskers twitched anxiously. "They took away the vending machines, didn't they? Holy cheeseballs! Where will we get our snacks from?"

Fuzzy shook his head. "It's not the vending machines. It's a teacher. An awful, horrible, no-good substitute teacher."

"Awww, you got a mean sub," said Igor the green iguana. "Boo-flippin'-hoo."

"Now, Brother Igor," Cinnabun chided. "Is that any way to support a fellow pet in need?" Their bunny president believed in fairness and team spirit (also in unicorns, but that was another story).

"Fuzzy needs to toughen up," said Igor, shifting on his pillow for comfort. "Everyone's had a dud sub. So what?"

"He's worse than a dud," said Fuzzy. "Mr. Brittle's a menace. He's already driven some of the students to tears, and it's just his first day."

Igor flapped a long-fingered hand. "Bah. Bad subs come and go, but class pets remain. Grow a thicker skin."

Mistletoe furrowed her brow. "I don't see what skin has to do with anything. Even if Fuzzy's hide was as thick as a rhino's, the substitute would still be mean."

"Figure of speech," said Igor, rolling his eyes.

"I'm not sure toughening up is the answer," said Marta. As the oldest class pet, the Russian tortoise had seen many seasons come and go at Leo Gumpus. "An unkind teacher can do permanent damage to a student."

"That's right," said Fuzzy. "We've got to protect the kids."

Cinnabun nodded. "Well, that is our sacred duty, after all."

"This sub is like nothing I've ever seen," said Fuzzy. "Has anyone had Mr. Brittle before?" The other pets shook their heads.

"You're making a mountain out of a molehill." Sassafras the parakeet groomed her wing calmly. "They let him teach—how bad could he be?"

"He called a student fat," said Fuzzy.

Mistletoe made a face. "That's rude."

"He whacks desks with a ruler if someone annoys him."

"That's uncalled for," said Marta.

"And . . . he wants to get rid of me," said Fuzzy.

The side chatter stopped. Every pet gave him their full attention.

"Get rid of a class pet?" Cinnabun chewed on a knuckle. "My stars, that sets a bad example. Subs can't do that, can they?"

"I don't know," said Fuzzy. "But he called me a disease-carrying distraction."

Igor smirked. "You do smell a little like rotten fruit."

Cinnabun shot the iguana an admonishing look.

"That's my shampoo," said Fuzzy.

Mistletoe paced. "This is dangersome. Very, very bad. If they dump you, they could get rid of any of us. I could be next!"

For the first time, Luther the rosy boa spoke up. "Hang loose, little mousie," he said. "When trouble comes, you gotta chill."

"Easy for you to say," said Fuzzy. "You're cold-blooded."

The snake slithered off his pillow. "All the same," he said, "we're not gonna fix this pickle if we lose our heads. Right?"

Fuzzy took a deep breath and blew it out. "You're right."

"Okay then, Fuzzmeister," said Luther. "Want to defeat your enemy?"

"Yeah!"

"Then you've gotta know your enemy. Fill us in on this subpar sub, Mr. Whoziewhatsit."

"Brittle, like the peanut." Fuzzy detailed all he'd observed about the man. When he finished, he looked around at his friends' faces. "So, what do you think?"

"*Hmm . . .*" said Marta, gnawing on a fruit chew.

"What does that mean?" said Fuzzy.

"It means . . . *hmm*," she said. "I've seen some bad subs in my time, but never one like this."

Reflectively scratching herself with a hind paw, Cinnabun asked, "You say he doesn't eat or drink, that he acts inhuman?"

"Yeah," said Fuzzy. "I'd swear he has no emotions except constant irritation."

There was much frowning and staring into the distance as everyone processed that idea. Then Mistletoe's face cleared. She sat bolt upright.

"I've got it," she said.

"Got what?" asked Igor. "The creeping crud?"

The mouse shook her head. "I know why he doesn't need food, why he shows no human feelings."

"End the suspense," said Cinnabun. "Tell us."

"Because he's not a human!" said the mouse triumphantly.

"Not a . . ." Fuzzy echoed.

"That's right," said Mistletoe. "Your substitute is a robot."

CHAPTER 3

Send In the Splash Squad

To say that the mouse's statement caused a stir would be like calling the Sahara a wee bit sandy. The clubhouse buzzed with the pets' reactions. Everyone had his or her own ideas on the subject, and for a minute, the space echoed with raised voices.

"A robot? No way!"

"Makes sense. I heard Principal Flake say she wanted to save money."

"Those machines freak me out!"

"Their only goal is world domination!"

Toonk, toonk, toonk! "Stop that carrying on!" The thump of the gavel finally brought some quiet to the room. Everyone turned to Cinnabun, who crouched on the presidential podium (actually *The Complete Works of William Shakespeare*) with a mallet in her paws.

"If y'all would just simmer down for a moment, we might get some actual thinking done here," she said. "Let's go one at a time. Sassafras?"

The parakeet bobbed with excitement. "First off, can I just say that robots are cool!"

"Not this robot," said Fuzzy. "He's a menace."

"I don't believe it," said Sassafras.

"Hey, it happens, baby," said Luther, looping his coils around a cat sculpture that had been rescued from the trash. "Just like with meals, there's good robots and bad robots."

Igor scoffed. "No such thing as a bad meal."

"Yeah!" echoed half of the pets in the room.

Holding up her paws, Cinnabun said, "Be that as it may, the subject was subs. Let's put this to a vote.

All in favor of helping Fuzzy drive off his evil robot substitute?"

"And save the students in my class," Fuzzy added.

One by one, every pet raised a paw, wing, front foot, or tail. Fuzzy's heart swelled with gratitude. His friends had his back.

"Marvelous," said the bunny. "We're all in agreement. Cast out the robot, protect the kids."

"Splendid," said Marta.

"Groovy," said Luther.

They all stared at one another for a moment.

Cinnabun spoke. "So . . . any idea how?"

The pets looked at one another some more. The silence was deafening.

"Push the robot's 'off' switch?" said Mistletoe at last.

Fuzzy cocked his head. "That might work. But what if we can't find the switch?"

"Um, take out its batteries?" said Marta.

"A robot would never let you do that," said Igor. "They're . . . whatchamacallit, self-protective."

The boa grinned. "So we creep up on him."

"Machines never rest," said Igor. "Hard to surprise something that doesn't sleep."

Luther rubbed his head on the cat sculpture. "Okay then, let's see . . . what if we annoy him so much, he leaves on his own?"

"I like that," said the iguana.

"You would," said Sassafras. "You're deeply annoying."

Igor stuck out his tongue at her, proving the parakeet's point.

Cinnabun gazed up at a corner of the clubhouse. "So what do robots hate?"

"The living?" said Fuzzy.

"No," said the bunny. "I mean, what's their weakness?"

"Beats me," said Sassafras, "but I can tell you a robot's favorite type of music."

Fuzzy frowned. "What's that?"

"Heavy metal!" the parakeet squawked.

He folded his arms. "I'm serious, Sassafras."

"Me too," she said. "Hey, you know why the robot had to go back to robot school?"

"No, why?" said Mistletoe, wide-eyed.

"Because its skills were getting a little rusty!" Sassafras cackled until she started coughing.

Luther groaned.

Fuzzy's irritation vanished as a thought popped into his head. "*Rusty?*" he said. "Hey, machines don't work so well if you get them wet, do they?"

Cinnabun smiled her dimpled smile. "No, they do not. In fact, they short-circuit or they rust. Why, what did you have in mind, Brother Fuzzy?"

"If only we could get him wet, that might stop our mean robot in his tracks," said Fuzzy.

"But how?" asked Marta.

"Push him into a swimming pool!" said Mistletoe.

"Blast him with squirt guns," said Igor.

Marta arched her brow. "And you don't think that might call a wee bit too much attention to us, dear?"

The iguana scowled.

"Sister Marta is right." Cinnabun daintily nibbled on a PowerBar. "Anything too obvious, and the humans might learn more about us than we want them to know. The jig, as they say, would be up."

"So we need to be sneaky," said Fuzzy.

Luther grinned. "I can do sneaky. We just keep ourselves incognito, that's all."

"In where?" asked Mistletoe.

"Hush-hush," said the snake. "You know, secret-like."

Fuzzy felt the tickle of an idea forming. He held up a paw. "What if," he said, "we could get him wet without showing ourselves at all?"

Luther nodded. "I hear what you say, baby. And I dig it."

"You mean, like, hide somewhere and splash him when he comes by?" asked Igor with a lazy smirk. "You're craftier than I thought, little pig."

"Rodent," said Fuzzy.

Cinnabun licked a paw and groomed her cheek

with it. "But we can't simply lurk behind a door. It would have to be someplace where the robot couldn't spot us, in case we miss."

One corner of Fuzzy's mouth quirked up. "Just leave that part to me," he said.

It took quite a while to put everything in place, but by bedtime that evening, Fuzzy was satisfied that all was ready. Tomorrow would tell whether their plan would work.

The next morning, the evil robot substitute was just as stiff, just as mean as the day before. Meaner, maybe. Because when it came time for the students to attend their enrichment class, Mr. Brittle stopped them as they began rising from their seats.

"Where do you think you are going?" he asked.

"This is our specials period," said Zoey-with-the-braces. "We've got music class with Mrs. Tucker."

The substitute scowled. "Not anymore. Sit back down."

"But—" Malik began.

"Music," sneered the sub, "is a thorough and complete waste of time."

Now Fuzzy *knew* the man was a robot. No human he'd ever met could resist the charms of music. Heck, even Fuzzy liked listening to the jazz that Miss Wills played on weekends at home, and he was a guinea pig.

"But Mrs. Tucker is expecting us," said Natalia, pushing her oversized glasses up the bridge of her nose. "And we love the class."

"You may as well learn to speak Ancient Greek," said Mr. Brittle, "for all the good it will do you. Music is worthless. Nobody ever got rich making music."

"What about the Beatles and the Rolling Stones?" asked Diego, who loved classic rock.

"The *Beatles*?" said the substitute. "Could you be any more ignorant and still know how to breathe? *Hmm?*"

Diego folded in on himself. Fuzzy's heart went out to him.

"Those are the exceptions that prove the rule." The robot teacher paced stiffly in front of the room. "For every Beatle or Beyoncé or Justin Bieber, there are tens of thousands—hundreds of thousands— of starving musicians. Why would anyone in his right mind want to play music?"

"Because it's fun?" squeaked Nervous Lily.

"*Fun?*" snapped Mr. Brittle. "School is not supposed to be fun. Forget music. Instead, we will do something productive."

"What do you mean?" asked Connor warily.

The robot sub raked his gaze over the classroom. "I am about to teach you something you will use for the rest of your lives."

"Comparison shopping?" said Maya.

"Accounting," said Mr. Brittle.

The students traded puzzled looks. "What's accounting?" asked Connor. "Is that like a-one, and a-two, and a-three?"

Shaking his head in disgust, the sub said, "You are without a doubt the dimmest bunch of brats I have ever taught. Accounting is the recording and summarizing of financial transactions."

Fuzzy could see shoulders sag and heads droop across the room. All except pigtailed Sofia, who said, "Does it involve numbers?"

"Nothing but," said Mr. Brittle.

Her smile widened. "I love math."

"As well you should," said the sub. "Let us begin."

Though it felt like it lasted longer than the Paleozoic Era, their accounting lesson stretched all the way until recess. Fuzzy, who was not a Numbers Rodent, found himself yawning and fighting sleep. When the kids escaped to the playground, Mr. Brittle stayed at his desk, as Fuzzy had expected.

Then came the tricky part.

If Fuzzy left his cage to help with the dousing, the sub would know that he could escape. Not good. So instead, he had to be the lookout while several of his fellow pets sneaked out of their rooms and splashed the substitute.

It wasn't that he didn't trust his friends. But Fuzzy didn't like to watch—he liked to *do*.

Round and round he paced, staring up at the ceiling. Where were they? Recess lasted only twenty minutes, and already ten minutes had passed.

The splash squad was late.

Fuzzy tugged his whiskers in a spasm of worry. If they didn't arrive soon, the other pets wouldn't be able to creep back into their cages before everyone returned to class. He ground his teeth. The waiting was killing him. No offense to Sassafras, but being a mere observer was for the birds.

Then, his ears twitched. A stealthy scraping came from above as the ceiling tile over the desk slid out of place.

Mr. Brittle frowned, stopped scribbling, and began to look around.

Wiggling whiskers! If he spotted the pets in the ceiling, it was all over.

"Hey!" Fuzzy shouted. "Mr. Robot! Over here!"

The sub swiveled his head toward the cage. Even

though he couldn't understand Fuzzy's language, it was plain to see that the noise bothered him.

"Shut your piehole, piggy," growled Mr. Brittle.

Beneath his words, Fuzzy detected a clatter as the pets wrestled the pail into place. The robot sub must have heard it too, as he again began to crane his neck and search for the source of the noise.

Desperate, Fuzzy jumped up and down, squeaking, "I'm a rodent, you bucket of bolts! Can't you even keep your animals straight?"

Mr. Brittle's scowl deepened as his gaze returned to the cage. "You are getting on my last nerve, you furry meatloaf." He stood, clenching his fists.

Uh-oh. Fuzzy gripped his cage bars. If the sub took even one step away from the desk, the pets above him would miss.

What was a guinea pig to do?

CHAPTER 4

Operation Wet Robot

Instantly, Fuzzy stopped yelling, dropped to all fours, and pasted the saddest, sorriest expression he could manage onto his face. At the sight of this, Mr. Brittle hesitated for a second.

That was all it took.

SSSPLOOOSH! A bucketful of water cascaded down onto the robot sub, drenching him wetter than an otter's pocket.

Mr. Brittle's eyes flew wide with shock; his shoulders hunched. "Wh-what the—?" he spluttered.

By the time he'd wiped the water from his eyes and checked out the ceiling, the tile was back in place. Score one for the splash squad!

Fuzzy tumbled over onto his back, laughing. With those wet clothes plastered to his skinny frame, the sub looked just like a scarecrow after a storm.

"Hey!" Mr. Brittle yelled at the ceiling. "Who is up there? I will have your hide for this!"

But no one answered. The pets had scurried away.

Cursing a blue streak, the robot sub shook water

off his arms and torso. He mopped his wet desktop with his equally wet jacket. But that must not have satisfied him. With a glance at the clock, he bolted out the door, *squelch-squish-squelch-squish*. Fuzzy was completely forgotten.

Chuckling to himself, Fuzzy replayed the splash in his mind. That was one wet robot! How long did it take a machine to rust? he wondered. Since they hadn't covered that in fifth-grade science, he could only guess.

As the students trickled back in from recess, Fuzzy entertained himself by imagining how the robot would wind down. Would it be all at once in midsentence—"Now, children, it's timmme forrrr *blurrrgh* . . ."—or slowly, minute by minute?

The bell rang. Since their teacher hadn't returned, kids roamed freely about, chatting with friends.

Then the door swung open. Mr. Brittle stalked into the room, glowering like a robot gunslinger. His shoes squelched when he walked, and his pants clung damply to his legs, but up top he wore a dry, yellow Leo Gumpus Elementary T-shirt with its goofy-looking lion mascot.

Not for nothing, but Fuzzy had always wondered why a school so far from Africa would choose a lion as its symbol. Why not something more appropriate, like a possum, a squirrel, or, best of all, a guinea pig?

Humans were a mystery.

Squish-squish-squish. The sub marched to the front of the room as students scrambled for their assigned seats. Vibrating with indignation like an angry tuning fork, he stopped beside the desk.

"Are you okay, Mr. Brittle?" asked Sofia.

"If I find that any of you little monsters are responsible for what happened," the sub snarled, "you will howl for your mothers."

"Responsible for what?" asked Malik.

"Somebody splashed me." Mr. Brittle's tone simmered with danger. "And I will not rest until I find out who."

Mystified, the students looked at one another. Fuzzy caught Spiky Diego stifling a smile. Mr. Brittle noticed it too.

"You with the hair," he said. "Did you do this?"

"No, sir," said the boy.

The robot sub's eyes narrowed. "I do not believe you. This is just the kind of prank that you would pull."

"I didn't do it," Diego muttered, hanging his head. Fuzzy felt a pang at seeing the boy falsely accused, but he could hardly confess to planning the drenching himself. After all, the sub didn't speak guinea pig.

"You think you are so smart, *hmm?*" said Mr. Brittle.

Diego's "No" was almost inaudible.

"Come stand before the class and give us a full report on the accrual method of accounting."

The corners of Diego's mouth pulled downward. "But I don't know the cruel method."

The sub sneered. "Then go stand in the corner. Class, open your science textbooks to page sixty-five."

Diego shuffled to the back of the room and stood there, shoulders slumped. Even his spiky hair looked sad.

"Turn around," said Mr. Brittle. "I do not want to look at that face."

As Diego twisted away from the class with a little sigh, the sub began the lesson.

Fuzzy hissed. Nobody got away with treating one of his students like that. It was going to be so sweet to witness the evil robot's downfall. He watched keenly for signs of rust or a short circuit. Nothing. Mr. Brittle carried on in his machinelike way, not missing a beat.

A few minutes later, Mr. Darius entered carrying a ladder and bucket. The sub ordered him to mop up the rest of the water and then check the crawl space for traces of the prankster. Mr. Brittle supervised the work with pursed lips. After taking care of the puddles, the custodian shone his flashlight around the drop ceiling, sneezed once, and descended the ladder.

"Well?" demanded Mr. Brittle. "What did you find?"

"Just some scrape marks in the dust," said Mr. Darius. "No way could a kid have gotten up there."

"And why not?"

Indicating the ceiling, the janitor said, "The tiles are too flimsy. A person—even a little kid—would fall right through."

The robot *suh harrumphed*. "Clearly *somebody* was up there, because somebody dumped that water on me. Is everyone at this school utterly incompetent?"

In a tone as chilly as winter wind Mr. Darius replied, "*Some* of us do our jobs just fine. Go on, crawl up there yourself, and see how quickly you fall through."

Mr. Brittle just snarled in response, making a shooing gesture with the backs of his hands. With great dignity, the custodian collected his ladder and bucket, nodded to the students, and left the room.

Fuzzy gnawed on a corner of his block, a habit that helped him think. This must be a fancy robot indeed, if the water didn't have any effect on it. He'd have to try another tack. Maybe he could find that "off" switch after all? Fuzzy decided to try.

As lessons resumed, he waited for his chance. Near the end of lunchtime, it came.

CHAPTER 5

Piggy Prison

A handful of kids had returned to class early and were quietly entertaining themselves under Mr. Brittle's watchful eye. Natalia, in the front row, had brought Fuzzy out of his cage for a cuddle. When Zoey with-the-braces began chatting with her, Natalia's attention wandered.

Gingerly, Fuzzy stepped out of her arms onto her desktop. Natalia didn't notice.

"No way," she told Zoey. "So what did your parents say then?"

"Well," said Zoey, "you wouldn't believe . . ."

Fuzzy eyeballed the gap between Natalia's desk and the teacher's. If he got up enough steam, he thought he could leap it.

Probably.

Maybe.

He checked on the girls: still chatting. He checked on the teacher: paging through a textbook.

A better chance might never come. Fuzzy did a couple of deep knee bends, took a couple of deep breaths. He glanced over the edge. *Yikes!* Natalia's desktop seemed pretty high up. What if he didn't jump far enough?

Fuzzy's stomach quaked like he'd swallowed a bellyful of bees. His whiskers quivered. *Don't think about it*, he told himself. *Just do it*. Clenching his teeth, Fuzzy crouched. Then, in an explosive burst, he dashed across Natalia's desktop and leaped into space.

Time slowed. Fuzzy noticed the wood grain of the desk ahead of him, the perfectly aligned papers on top of it. He also noted again how *really far down* the floor was.

Holy haystacks!

As his jump began to lose momentum, Fuzzy stretched his front paws out as far as they would go. But would it be far enough?

His body sank lower, lower. With a last desperate twitch, Fuzzy reached for the edge of the teacher's desk and just caught it with his front claws.

Whoomp! His body slammed into the side of the desk like a sack of bowling balls, knocking the wind clear out of him. But his grip held.

Fuzzy was vaguely aware of the girls squealing. Ignoring them, he scrabbled with his hind legs, dug into the wood with his claws, and dragged himself onto the desk. *Whew!*

Mr. Brittle had half risen from his chair. His hands still rested on the desktop. Before the man could move away, Fuzzy sprinted across the papers. Onto the sub's clammy hand and up his arm he scuttled.

"Eeek!" shrieked Mr. Brittle, displaying an impressively high range for a male robot. His other hand rose to sweep Fuzzy away.

Dodging around the outside of the upper arm, Fuzzy just managed to duck the brush-off. In another second, he'd reached the shoulder. Mr. Brittle jolted fully upright, wiggling and waggling like a deranged break-dancer to dislodge his attacker.

"Get it off, get it off!" he yelped.

Kids hurried forward to help the sub.

Now, where's that power button? Fuzzy wondered. He scurried across the robot's writhing shoulder, which pitched like a houseboat in a hurricane, and finally reached the collar. He tugged on the teacher's ear.

Nothing. With frantic paws, Fuzzy groped up and down the neck, searching for that button.

Still nothing. Just a smooth stretch of warm flesh that turned stubbly up by the hairline. Mr. Brittle giggled and twitched. "*Aah!* Get it off! It tickles!"

Before Fuzzy could dive down under the shirt and investigate further, a hand closed around him. In a flash, he was lifted away.

"Nooo!" cried Fuzzy. "Put me down—I wasn't done yet!"

He struggled, but it was useless. Someone—Natalia, he saw—had him in a secure, two-handed grip.

"Easy now," she cooed. "It's going to be all right. Nothing to be scared of."

"I'm gonna fry that pig!" cried Mr. Brittle.

Well, almost *nothing*, thought Fuzzy.

Shielding him with her body, Natalia edged around the substitute and over to the cage. "You don't under-stand!" Fuzzy cried. "He's a dangerous robot!" But the girl just stroked his fur and set him down gently on the pine shavings.

"Too much excitement, Mr. Fuzzy," she cooed. "Get some rest now."

Rearing onto his hind legs, Fuzzy gripped the bars. His heart hammered faster than an octopus carpenter on a deadline. How could he have missed the robot sub's "off" switch? Was it hidden somewhere? And what kind of robot had warm skin, anyway?

As Fuzzy agonized, Mr. Brittle collected two stray cafeteria trays from the worktable. With a grim expression, he stalked up to the cage.

Natalia raised a protective hand. "Don't hurt him!"

"No worries," said Mr. Brittle. "Much as I might like to, I do not intend to squish your little 'friend.'"

"Good." Natalia relaxed a little.

"But enough is enough. No more snuggles. From now on, he stays in piggy jail." And with a *whock-whock*, the sub slapped the trays down side by side, covering the cage's open top. Then he weighted them down with textbooks.

"No!" cried Fuzzy. Taking away his cuddles was cruel and unusual punishment for a guinea pig. Worse than that, it just wasn't right.

Bending down until they were nose to nose, Mr. Brittle blasted Fuzzy with a dose of stale garlic breath. "No more playtime, furball. You stay put."

The man-robot-whatever squelched his way back to his desk and called the class to order. As Mr. Brittle began analyzing the life out of what used to be a fun book, Fuzzy fumed. It wasn't fair! The sub couldn't just lock him up like that, could he?

Miss Wills would never treat him so harshly. But then, Miss Wills was gone. And who knew when she might be coming back?

Fuzzy and his students might be stuck with the Worst Sub in the History of the Universe for a long, long time.

CHAPTER 6

Flake Out

Through the rest of that endless afternoon, Fuzzy moped and grumped, barely stirring in his cage. He was fast running out of ideas to stop this unstoppable teacher.

So when Principal Flake showed up right after class ended, his heart gave a little leap. The principal, as every class pet knows, is the most powerful person at school. If Fuzzy could only communicate the sub's awfulness to her, Mrs. Flake would boot him out the door in a hot minute.

"Oh, Mrs. Flake!" Fuzzy chirped, waving his paws. "Over here!"

She didn't notice. She only had eyes for Mr. Brittle.

As solidly built as a small truck, Mrs. Kimberly Flake had electric-blue eyes and hair that reminded Fuzzy of petrified hay—a mix of yellow, tan, and gray that not even a gale-force wind could stir. She trundled right up to the desk.

"Mr. Brittle," she said. "Might I have a word?"

The substitute glanced up from his papers with an expression as deadpan as a frozen dingo. "Yes?"

"I have heard reports of students being mistreated in your classroom," said the principal. "Disturbing reports."

"That's right!" chirped Fuzzy.

"You know how kids exaggerate," said the teacher, jotting a note.

Fuzzy bristled. "They're not exaggerating at all!"

Folding her arms, the principal said, "Children in tears, children being bullied, children complaining that you canceled their music class. These are serious charges, Mr. Brittle."

"Give it to him!" Fuzzy cried.

The substitute stifled a yawn. "Is that all?"

His reaction made the principal scowl. "That's more than enough to get a teacher dismissed. What do you have to say for yourself?"

The man sneered up at her. "Two words: teacher shortage."

Principal Flake blinked.

"Nobody wants this crummy job." Mr. Brittle began packing up his papers and books. "You would be hard-pressed to find another substitute, especially on short notice."

"I don't—" the principal began.

"And besides, my contract protects me. As long as I do not strike the students, you will have a hard time dismissing me."

Mrs. Flake gaped like a baby bird that's missed its mealtime. "That's not—"

"Furthermore, you might have to hire me full time after you dismiss Miss Wills." The substitute calmly stowed his papers in his messenger satchel.

The principal's scowl deepened. "And why on earth would I dismiss one of my best teachers?"

"Neglect of duty." Mr. Brittle sniffed. "It is in the handbook, paragraph 214-b. I would say skipping class qualifies."

"That's ridiculous. She's on *jury duty*!"

"I am sure the superintendent will appreciate my point of view. He is my second cousin, after all."

"But—"

The sub stood. "And now, if you will excuse me, I am late for an appointment." Collecting his bag and jacket, Mr. Brittle marched stiffly to the door, where he turned and offered a wintry smile. "Nice chatting with you."

"Nooo!" cried Fuzzy.

After casting a curious glance at the trays atop Fuzzy's cage, the principal sighed and followed the substitute out of the room.

Fuzzy bit his lip. Could the sub really get Miss Wills fired? And if he did, what would that mean for a certain classroom pet? Would Fuzzy be out in the cold?

His head whirled at the thought. He could expect no help from on high—even the principal was powerless against this monster. Fuzzy and the other pets would need to get *really* creative if they wanted to save the students of 5-B.

But first, thought Fuzzy, staring up at the trays that held him trapped in his home, *I've got to get out of here.*

Fortunately, Mr. Darius didn't hold the same views on rodent imprisonment as the substitute did. When he came to clean up the room that afternoon, the custodian removed the trays and books from atop Fuzzy's domain.

"That's no way to treat a pet," he said. "And besides, these belong back in the cafeteria."

Fuzzy heaved a sigh of relief. "Thanks, Mr. Darius!" he squeaked.

The janitor petted him and shared a carrot chunk. "Your sub is a piece of work, little buddy," he said, shaking his head. "Sorry, but I think you guys will have to grin and bear it."

Fuzzy chuffed in disgust.

Mr. Darius chuckled. "I hear you, amigo. Wish there was something I could do to help."

He went about his business, tidying up and emptying the trash. When at last the custodian shut the door with a parting "Hang in there!" Fuzzy was raring to visit the clubhouse.

In a matter of minutes he'd escaped his cage and entered the crawl space above the ceiling. Fuzzy trotted along toward the club meeting, bristling with purpose and indignation like a ticked-off porcupine. They simply had to find another way to oust that awful sub.

They *had* to.

When at last he hurried down the ramp, the clubhouse rang with laughter and chatter. Everyone but

Marta was present. Sassafras perched on the cat statue, reenacting their prank.

"And then, we let 'er rip!" the parakeet crowed. "Bam! Splash! Bull's-eye!"

"Hey, Fuzzarino!" Luther greeted him. "Was it sweet watching that robot run down? Wish I could've been there, baby."

Fuzzy frowned. "Bad news."

"Someone canceled your subscription to *Hay and Horsegrass Magazine*?" Igor teased.

"Nope. It didn't work."

"Say wha-a-at?" drawled Luther.

The other pets crowded around. "I'm as lost as last year's Easter egg," said Cinnabun. "How could it not work? We drenched that robot but good!"

"Worse news," said Fuzzy. "He's not a robot."

"But—the way he acted?" said Mistletoe.

Fuzzy shook his head. "He didn't rust or short-circuit. I climbed all over him looking for a power button. Nothing."

"So he's . . . really not a robot?" said Sassafras.

"His skin was warm; he's human," said Fuzzy.

Deflated, the bird turned away. "Dang. It would've been so cool . . ."

"Well, that just frosts my pumpkin," said the bunny.

The enthusiasm leaked from the room like the air from an inflatable kiddie pool, leaving soggy disappointment in its wake. A couple of the pets shuffled over to their pillows and flopped down.

"This isn't over," said Fuzzy.

"What do you mean?" Mistletoe pouted. "We failed."

With a wave of his arms, Fuzzy said, "Don't you get it? He may not be a robot, but he's still a terrible human."

"Amen to that." Cinnabun slumped against the presidential podium.

"Mr. Brittle wants to get rid of Miss Wills," said Fuzzy. "And if he does, I might be next."

Mistletoe gasped. "No! He can't!"

"We don't know what he can do," said Fuzzy. "That's why we've got to force him to leave, before it's too late."

The bunny toyed with one of her floppy ears. "So what do you propose?"

"I, uh . . ." Fuzzy threw up his paws. "I'm not sure. I need everyone's help on this. What makes humans move?"

Mistletoe perked up. "Ooh, I know! Music!"

"He hates music," said Fuzzy.

The mouse sagged. "Oh."

"Money," said Igor. "Humans are crazy fond of money."

Sassafras cocked her head. "So we pay him to make him leave?"

"Sure, why not?" The iguana shrugged.

"Just one small problem I can see," said Fuzzy.

"What's that?" said Igor.

"We have no money."

Igor gave a slow blink. "Way to rain on my parade."

Fuzzy appealed to the rest of the pets. "Come on. There's got to be another way to get rid of this guy."

"Charm?" said Cinnabun. Dimples bloomed in her cheeks as she smiled.

Fuzzy frowned. "I can't charm the guy—he hates me."

"I wasn't talking about *you*," said the bunny.

Stroking his chin, Fuzzy asked, "Okay, so you charm him. How would that work, exactly?"

"First, I sashay on in there." Cinnabun demonstrated her words.

"Ooh," said Mistletoe. "That's the cutest sashay I've ever seen!"

"And then, when his defenses are down, I give him a Force Five Adorability Attack." The bunny wound her paws together, lifted her shoulders, and batted her big brown eyes.

"Awww," said every pet in the room except Fuzzy.

Much as it might annoy him, Fuzzy couldn't deny her appeal. "Your cuteness is . . . uh, impressive," he said. "But how will you charm him into leaving if you can't speak human?"

"He's right," said the mouse. "One look at you, and the sub would want to stay forever."

Cinnabun dropped her pose like a bad habit. "Well, swat my hind with a melon rind. I hadn't thought of that."

For a long stretch, nobody said anything. They just

stared into space, thoroughly stumped. Then Luther grinned a snaky grin.

"It's time to break out our number-one secret weapon," he said.

"What's that?" asked Igor. "Piggy poop?"

The boa shook his head. "Fear."

"Fear?" echoed Fuzzy. "How do you mean?"

Gracefully slithering into the center of the room, Luther said, "Look, what are humans most afraid of?"

"Death?" said Igor.

"Oral reports?" said Sassafras.

"Missing out on the last cookie in the box?" said Mistletoe.

Luther's smile widened. "*Sssnakesss*, baby," he hissed.

The other pets stared at him, struck by the idea. Then, heads began to nod.

"I like it," said Fuzzy. "It could work."

"Tonight, me and Fuzzanova go back to his room," said the boa. "Then, I hide someplace guaranteed to give maximum shock. When that nasty dude sees me, bimmity-bam-boom! It's good-bye, sub; hello, peace of mind."

The thing with plans, Fuzzy thought the next morning while waiting for the teacher to arrive, *is that you never know how well they'll work*. He paced the length of his cage and checked the clock. Not long now.

"You okay in there?" he called out.

"As cool as polar bear buns," came Luther's muffled voice from the desk. "We're good to go."

At long last, something clattered in the lock, and the door swung open. Mr. Brittle marched into the room, trailing his own personal cloud of gloom. Fuzzy tracked his every move.

When he noticed the attention, the sub said, "Stop staring, you furry potato." Then he did a double take. "Where is your roof? That worthless janitor is in so much trouble."

As Mr. Brittle crossed to the desk, Fuzzy reared up on his hind legs to watch. The man removed his jacket, unpacked his messenger bag, and sat down.

Any second now, Fuzzy thought. He felt tingly all over. *This is going to be* epic!

But the sub didn't open the desk drawer. Instead, he studied the books and papers spread before him, tapping the eraser end of a pencil against his square little teeth.

Come on, come on, thought Fuzzy.

Students shuffled in and lessons began, but still the sub didn't even touch the drawer. The morning dragged on. But if it was torture for Fuzzy, it was even worse for the students.

First, Mr. Brittle canceled their creative writing project. "A frivolous waste of time." Then he insulted Heavy-Handed Jake. "Honestly, are you *trying* to be the dumbest kid at school?" The sub even refused to continue Miss Wills's read-aloud tradition. "Why should I do your work for you? You will never be better readers if you do not actually read."

Fuzzy ground his teeth in an agony of impatience. The one thing the sub didn't do was open the desk.

Finally, just before recess, his ballpoint ran dry. Mr. Brittle scanned the desktop. "Where does your teacher keep her spare pens?" he demanded of Messy Mackenzie.

"In the top drawer," said the girl.

At last! Fuzzy gripped the bars of his cage, and his mouth curled into a grin.

This was going to be good.

CHAPTER 7

Hide and Go "Eek!"

As Mr. Brittle pulled open the drawer, Fuzzy heard a faint hiss

The reaction was immediate.

"*Yahhh!*" screamed the sub. His eyes went as round as volleyballs, and his mouth opened wide enough to accommodate small aircraft. Mr. Brittle shoved the wheeled chair away from the desk so hard, he went over backward with a thud.

Wheek-wheek! Fuzzy jumped straight up with excitement. "Take that!" he cried.

Several helpful students rushed to Mr. Brittle's side and tried to help him up. "What's wrong?" asked Sofia.

Swatting their hands away, the sub snarled, "Back off, you monsters! You think you can prank me, then turn around and help me? *Hmm?*"

"Prank you?" said Malik.

The teacher climbed to his feet, eyes blazing. "I know who put that snake there."

Malik and Sofia exchanged puzzled glances. "Snake?" she said. "We didn't—"

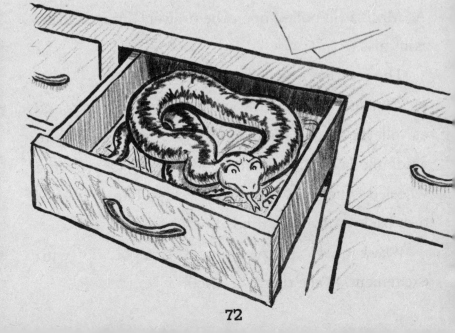

"No more lies!" snapped Mr. Brittle. "No more tricks. This thing just got serious."

The students cried out, protesting their innocence. But the substitute snatched his ruler off the desktop—steering well clear of the open drawer—and shook it at them.

"I am a teacher," he snarled. "You should be respectful and obedient. Instead, you treat me like this." He thrust the straightedge at Luther's drawer.

The recess bell rang. Students got up to leave.

"Sit your little heinies down!" roared the sub. "You are not going anywhere."

"But—" Loud Brandon began.

"Recess is canceled until further notice!"

"Nooo!" cried the kids. Fuzzy gasped. Luther had goofed—the fear approach was only making things worse!

Mr. Brittle's face turned an interesting shade of crimson. He spat out his words like bullets. "Sit. *Down*. Everyone."

Sulky and reluctant, the students obeyed.

"Now, *you*"—the sub jabbed the ruler at Heavy-Handed Jake—"go tell the janitor to remove that snake. I am giving everyone twenty pages of homework tonight."

The students groaned, but there was nothing they could do. Right away, Mr. Brittle launched into another accounting lesson. They had no choice but to follow along.

As Jake left on his errand, Fuzzy scanned the room. Zoey-with-the-braces had laid her head on her desk. Brandon and Lily trembled, near tears. Aside from math-loving Sofia and Gabe, the rest of the students seemed lower than a centipede's belt buckle.

Fuzzy hissed in frustration. Water didn't work. Fear didn't work. Even the mighty principal had failed. Was there no way to drive out this sinister substitute?

After school, the Class Pets' clubhouse was nearly as gloomy as the atmosphere in Room 5-B. Luther nibbled listlessly on a PowerBar as Cinnabun tried to lighten his mood.

"It's gone," the boa told her. "All gone."

"What is?" she asked.

"I couldn't scare him off. I've losssst my mojo."

The bunny patted a muscular coil. "Fiddlesticks," she said. "You're just as scary as ever."

"You're only saying that."

"Not in the least," said Cinnabun. "Why, Mistletoe is plumb terrified of you."

"I really am," the mouse put in kindly.

Luther rested his chin on the snack and sighed. "No usssse trying to cheer me up."

"You know the worst part?" Fuzzy raised his head from the pillow where he'd sprawled.

"Worse than having scare tactics backfire?" said Sassafras.

"Okay, maybe the just-as-awful part," said Fuzzy. "It's the students' morale. In three days, they've gone from bright kids excited about learning to sad mopes who just don't care. And there's no sign of Miss Wills coming back."

Cinnabun tut-tutted. "Poor little angels," she said. "There must be some way we can lift their spirits."

"Let's put on a show!" chirped Sassafras in a burst of enthusiasm. "A little song, a little dance, a little razzle-dazzle. They'll be smiling again in no time."

"Great idea, except for one thing," said Igor, popping a grape into his mouth.

"What's that?" asked the parakeet.

"It's a terrible idea." The iguana ticked off the reasons on three of his long fingers. "First, if we leave our classrooms to perform for the kids, everyone will know we can break out of our cages. Not good. Second, they'll wonder who could have trained all of us to put on a show. Also not good."

"And third?" asked Marta.

Igor scowled. "I don't dance."

Cinnabun hopped up onto the presidential podium. "Enough moping, y'all. As your thoroughly adorable president, I call this meeting to order!"

The pets sat up straighter (except for Luther, who still sprawled) and gave her their attention.

"First off, I move we jump right past old business and start with new business," said the bunny.

"I second that," said Mistletoe.

All the pets agreed, and so Cinnabun continued. "Our job—no, our *calling*—is to bring joy into children's lives, is that not so?"

"You got that right," said Luther, rallying a bit.

"So if we can't entertain the little darlings, as Brother Igor has so helpfully pointed out—"

"I live to serve," said the iguana.

"We'll have to bring joy in a *sneakier* fashion," said Cinnabun.

Luther's head rose. "Did someone mention my favorite word?"

"Um, what did you have in mind?" asked Fuzzy.

He wanted to cheer up the kids, but he knew the bunny tended to go overboard with the cutesy-wutesy stuff.

"Love notes," said Cinnabun.

"But it's not Valentine's Day," said Mistletoe.

Their bunny president sent the mouse a sugary smile. "And why should love be limited to just one day a year?"

Mistletoe looked to Fuzzy, who shrugged. Cinnabun had a point.

"Love notes," said the rabbit, "will remind the kids that they are precious, delightful people, no matter what this so-called teacher says."

Fuzzy nodded slowly. Syrupy she might be, but Cinnabun's statement was true. "I get you. Anonymous notes, maybe?"

"Slipped into their desks," said Cinnabun.

Igor's face lit up with a wicked grin. "And while we're at it, I've got a great idea about something we can slip into Mr. Creepazoid's desk."

"All in favor?" said Cinnabun.

"Aye!" shouted the pets.

With twinkling eyes, she sized up the group. "Then what are we waiting for, y'all? Let's get gooey!"

CHAPTER 8

Rock the Note

For the next few hours, mushiness ruled the clubhouse. But that wasn't to say that the course of love ran smoothly. Although all the animals could read to varying degrees, writing was another matter entirely. Still, they gamely gathered colored paper, and with crayons held in paws, mouths, or coils, they set to work. Painstakingly, the pets scrawled messages like:

You are a good person, and

People really, really like you, and

No matter what that stinker says, you're a smart cookie.

After decorating the messages with little hearts, the pets carried them through the crawl space to Room 5-B. Every kid's desk received a note, except for Diego's, which got three. (Fuzzy thought he needed extra encouragement.)

Over Cinnabun's objections, Igor, Fuzzy, and Sassafras each left a little surprise in Mr. Brittle's top drawer.

"After all," said the iguana, "we haven't tried grossing him out yet."

Fuzzy wasn't sure this tactic would work, but he had to admit it felt satisfying. Everyone wished him good night, and the other pets headed for their own classrooms, worn out from the long day.

But before Sassafras left, Fuzzy pulled her aside to ask a favor. Just in case the gross-out trick fell short, he wanted to have a backup plan in place. After all, this substitute had proved to be harder to get rid of than a case of mange mites, and a wise rodent is always prepared for anything.

The next day dawned cloudy and gray as a wolf's wardrobe. Before the students arrived, Fuzzy ran a few laps around the cage and chased his ball. He wanted to be full of energy and ready for whatever the day would bring.

Mr. Brittle turned up first, no surprise there. He followed the same routine as the previous day, down to ordering Fuzzy not to stare at him. As before, he didn't open his desk drawer but started in with the textbooks and his smartphone.

In ones and twos, students trudged into class. Fuzzy watched as first this one, then that one found their notes. A warm feeling, sweet as sunshine, spread through his chest as their eyes brightened and smiles bloomed. It was almost like the good old days of last week, before the sub troubles began.

Bit by bit, with each note discovered, Fuzzy felt the room's spirits lift. Amazing what a little love can do. Kids were looking around, asking one another who had left the messages. Nobody knew. When he discovered his stash, Spiky Diego grinned from ear to ear. Fuzzy cherished a secret smile.

But he should've known it was too good to last.

Just after the first bell rang, Mr. Brittle noticed the colorful scraps of paper in his students' hands and their wide grins. His eyes narrowed. "What's all this?" he asked Natalia.

She held up her message. "Somebody left me—left us—the sweetest notes."

The sub leaned over his desk, his dark eyes scanning the words. "*Hmph*. It seems that someone with terrible handwriting is trying to spread good cheer." A strange expression, almost like hope, flashed across his face. "Let's see if they left me something too."

For just a second, Fuzzy felt sorry that they were playing a mean trick on the man. But the feeling passed when he thought about how the sub was bullying the kids.

Easing back from his desk, Mr. Brittle slid out the drawer and reached inside. First puzzlement, then alarm, then utter disgust crossed his face.

"Who is responsible for this?" he thundered, wiping his hand on a blank sheet of paper.

"Didn't you get a love note?" asked Maya.

Face purpling with rage, the sub hustled over to the classroom sink, blasted the hot water, and began scrubbing his hand hard enough to peel the paint off a small battleship.

"What is it?" asked Connor.

"You know perfectly well what it is," he snarled. "Feces! Fecal matter!"

"Huh?" said Heavy-Handed Jake, who was a bit behind on vocabulary words.

"Poop!" roared Mr. Brittle. "There's poop in my desk!"

Kids giggled. Fuzzy figured they couldn't help themselves.

"It's not funny!" the substitute snapped.

Actually it *was* kind of funny, and Fuzzy couldn't help snickering too, even though he felt a little bad for the man. But things didn't stay amusing for long.

"Who did this?" Wiping his reddened hands with a paper towel, Mr. Brittle stalked down the aisles, glaring right and left. "Was it you?"

"No!" said Brandon.

"You?" The sub accused Zoey-with-the-braces, who was having trouble controlling her giggles.

She covered her face and wordlessly shook her head.

"Or maybe it's been you all along, *hmm?*" Mr. Brittle snarled with silky menace, stopping directly in front of Spiky Diego.

The boy's eyes widened and he held up his palms. "It wasn't me, honest."

Fuzzy saw all the good feeling from the love notes melting away like sugar in a saucepan. His heart went out to the boy. This wasn't supposed to happen—the gross-out was supposed to make Mr. Brittle leave, not give him an excuse to torture more kids.

Everything was going horribly wrong.

"Think you can fool me, with your sneaky little face and your shifty little ways?" said the substitute. "You crept in here before school and left that mess, yes?"

"No," said Diego. "I don't have a key."

"Ha!" Mr. Brittle's eyes bulged. "You stole it. Your type always does."

"What do you mean, 'his type'?" Maya defended her friend. "Diego's no thief."

The sub wheeled on her. "And you are his partner in crime, is that it?"

"No!" Maya and Diego protested.

Baring his teeth, Mr. Brittle snapped, "Whether you did it or not, you two will scrub out my desk drawer."

"But—" Maya began.

"I want it spotless and feces-free." When the two of them just sat there staring, the teacher barked, "Now!"

Diego and Maya traded a quick glance, then rose from their chairs to follow his orders. Fuzzy slumped to his pine-shaving floor. His stomach knotted up like a first grader's shoelaces.

Mr. Brittle addressed the room. "Would someone like to confess?"

No one spoke. The students watched him with wide, worried eyes.

"Last chance," said the sub. "If no one confesses, I will have to punish everyone."

"Nooo!" the class moaned.

"Then you leave me no choice," said Mr. Brittle.

"Wh-what will you do to us?" Nervous Lily's voice shook.

The sub regarded the class for a long moment, hands on hips. A cruel light entered his eyes, and Fuzzy couldn't help trembling in sympathy for the kids.

"If you keep behaving like savages, you will be treated like savages," said Mr. Brittle. "Everyone, move your desks to the side of the room." When they gaped at him in confusion, the teacher snapped, "Do it!"

With much scraping and bumping, the students obeyed.

"Now, fetch your notebooks and pencils, and sit on the floor."

"But this is my favorite dress. It'll get dirty," Abby objected.

"I do not care," growled the sub. "Savages do not sit at nice desks. Savages sit on the ground."

Reluctantly, the kids retrieved their notebooks and sat on the floor. Fuzzy winced. Those cold tiles would feel really hard, really soon.

By this time, Spiky Diego and Maya had rejoined their classmates. After inspecting their work, Mr. Brittle scrawled something on two sheets of paper, snipped off a couple of lengths of twine, and taped one to each sheet in an upside-down U shape. He handed the pages to them.

"What's this?" asked Maya.

"Your punishment," said the sub. "Wear these all day long, so that everyone knows what you have done."

"But we didn't—" Maya began.

"I do not care. Since no one confessed, you will serve as an example to the rest." He pointed at Diego. "You with the hair, read yours aloud to the class."

The boy scanned his sheet and his face went gray. When he read, his voice was barely audible.

"Nice and loud," said the teacher. "Make them hear it in Poughkeepsie."

After clearing his throat, Diego read,

*"I am a rude, lying student who doesn't respect his
teacher.*

I deserve every punishment I get."

By the time he choked out the last few words,
Diego's voice quavered and his eyes were moist. Mr.
Brittle crossed his arms, nodding with a satisfied
smirk.

At this, Fuzzy's sympathy turned to ice-cold anger.
He bristled, rumbling deep in his chest. This man,
this so-called teacher, had gone way, *way* too far.

It was time to launch the backup plan.

Time to delve deep into the substitute's secrets and
find his weakness.

Time for Fuzzy's revenge.

CHAPTER 9

Stowaway Piggy

Like the reek of a dead rat in the attic, the effects of Mr. Brittle's punishment lingered throughout the day. He kept calling the students "savages" and treating them more and more barbarically.

Recess was canceled because "Savages do not play." The kids had to eat lunch off the cafeteria floor because "Savages do not use plates and tables."

And art class was called off because "Savages cannot appreciate the finer things."

After witnessing all this, Fuzzy thought that the true savage was Mr. Brittle himself. His nastiness took Fuzzy's breath away. The sub was the Mozart of meanness, the Cezanne of cruel. If nastiness were an Olympic sport, he would walk away with a fistful of gold medals.

By day's end, the kids were shuffling about in a state of shock, red-eyed and stoop-shouldered. Needless to say, very little learning took place that day.

When at last the students shambled out the door like the dazed survivors of a zombie apocalypse, Fuzzy was aching to put his plan into action. Pacing around his cage until he wore ruts in the pine shavings, he waited for Sassafras to arrive.

And waited.

Mr. Brittle lingered, doing whatever it is that teachers do after the kids have gone. But Fuzzy knew the sub wouldn't stick around much longer. Hoping the teacher wouldn't notice, he set up his ball, blocks, and platform to prepare for a quick escape.

But Sassafras still didn't show.

Fuzzy was gnawing his lip in frustration when he finally heard what he'd been waiting for.

"Mr. Brittle?" The faint voice came from outside the door. "Are you still there?"

The substitute frowned. "Who is it?"

"Miss Keet, one of the other teachers." Fuzzy felt giddy with relief, though he winced at the fake name Sassafras had chosen. *Keet*, as in parakeet? That bird did not have much of a future as an international spy.

"What do you want?" said Mr. Brittle. "I am busy."

Sassafras's voice turned honeyed. "I need the help of a big strong man like you."

"Can it wait?" The sub looked annoyed, which seemed to Fuzzy practically the sole expression he had.

"It'll only take a minute," said Sassafras, "and I'm just down the hall. Pleeease?"

Mr. Brittle rolled his eyes. "Try someone else," he called.

"The other men are gone. But anyway, everyone knows you're the strongest."

Fuzzy made a face. Sassafras was laying it on awfully thick. Would the sub take the bait?

"Pretty pleeease?" trilled the bird.

With a heavy sigh, the teacher stood. "Oh, all right. But this better be quick."

Fuzzy smirked. Some humans could be talked into anything.

Muttering to himself, Mr. Brittle marched to the door and peered out. "Miss Keet?" he said. "Where are you?"

Very faintly, Fuzzy could hear Sassafras down the hall. "Right this way, Mr. Brittle!" The door swung shut as the sub followed her voice.

In a flash, Fuzzy rocketed up onto the block, the ball, and then the platform. With a cry of "alley-oop!" he scrambled over the cage wall and crashed onto the table. Sassafras's trick wouldn't hold the sub for long; he had to hurry.

Bip-bop-boop—Fuzzy leaped from table to chair and slid down its leg to the floor. He cut a glance at the door. Still closed.

So far, so good.

Dashing like his feet were on fire, he dodged around the students' desks still crammed together on his side of the room. Fuzzy was just approaching the teacher's desk when he heard heels clicking down the hallway outside. It sounded like they'd almost reached the door!

With a final burst of speed, Fuzzy closed the distance. His goal: the substitute's messenger bag. He reached for the leather satchel, which dangled from the chair back . . .

And fell short.

Aw, cat doodies! Guinea pigs aren't the world's best jumpers, and the bag hung just a few inches too high for him to latch on to.

Someone fumbled with the doorknob. Mr. Brittle was returning!

Fuzzy's heart rat-a-tatted like a tap-dancing tarantula. Desperate, he cast about for something to stand on. A wicker wastebasket stood beside the desk.

No time to think. In one continuous movement, Fuzzy toppled the wastebasket, rolled it against the chair leg, and launched himself up onto it.

The door creaked open. Electrified with fright, Fuzzy lunged for the narrow opening at the top of the bag. As he leaped, the bin rolled away from under him.

Yikes! Fuzzy stretched to his limit, just managing to snag the satchel.

Thunk-thunk-thunk went Mr. Brittle's heavy footfalls against the checkerboard tiles. The desk would block Fuzzy from sight for another few seconds, but he had to move fast. Clinging to the lip of the bag with both paws, Fuzzy hauled himself up —he really *was* going to start doing chin-ups tomorrow—and jammed his head and shoulders under the flap.

The footsteps drew nearer as Fuzzy made one last titanic effort, pulling and wriggling for all he was worth. At last, he squeezed himself through the opening and tumbled to the bottom of the satchel. Instantly, he froze.

"Now, what . . . ?" Mr. Brittle's voice sounded very near. "How did this happen?"

Fuzzy guessed that the man had noticed the over-turned wastebasket.

"Must have kicked it when I got up," the sub muttered. "What a time waster—that ditz disappeared."

The inside of Mr. Brittle's bag smelled of old leather and eucalyptus. In the dimness, Fuzzy could just make out a packet of throat lozenges, along with a notepad, calculator, textbook, a few loose sheets, and a red apple. He heard a rustle of papers somewhere nearby and the faint *toonk-toonk* as the teacher rapped the edges on the desk to align them.

A jolt shot through him like he'd licked a light socket. Any second now, Mr. Brittle would shove his things into the messenger bag, and Fuzzy did not want to be discovered when he did. Lying down, he grabbed some paper and pulled it over him. It wasn't perfect, but it might hide him from a casual glance.

Sure enough, the satchel rocked as Mr. Brittle opened the flap and slid a sheaf of papers inside. Since the man said nothing, Fuzzy guessed his fur hadn't been spotted. He let out a long sigh of relief.

Then a heavy book landed on his back, and Fuzzy went "*Oof!*"

He froze. Had the substitute heard him?

"What the . . . ?" Mr. Brittle muttered.

Fuzzy clenched his jaw. It was all over now. As soon as the man plunged his hand into the bag, he'd find Fuzzy and return him to his cage. Probably he'd make the cage permanently escape-proof, then ship Fuzzy off to a pet store in Peru.

So much for the backup plan.

Beedle-deedle-dee. An electronic warble sounded.

"Yes?" said Mr. Brittle.

Fuzzy braced himself. Any second now that hand was coming . . .

"Uh-huh," said the sub. "I see. No, I ordered them in brown. B-R-O-W-N. What? No, check the order form. Are you blind as well as useless? *Hmm?*"

Amazingly, the bag's flap flopped down again, and the satchel lurched as it was lifted into the air.

When Mr. Brittle slung the bag over his shoulder, Fuzzy felt the thump in his back molars.

"Oh, really?" said the teacher. "I would like to talk with your supervisor. Yes, I would. You are not getting off that easy."

The satchel swayed as the substitute crossed the room, walked out the door, and locked it, talking all the while. Wriggling out from under the textbook, Fuzzy made himself as comfortable as he could.

Step one of his plan was complete.

Now came the hard part: ferreting out the secrets of the Meanest Sub in the Universe.

CHAPTER 10

Fuzzy the Spy

Fuzzy had heard Miss Wills use the saying *familiarity breeds contempt*, but he'd never understood it. Until now. The more time Fuzzy spent with Mr. Brittle, the less he liked him. (Which was tricky, since he hadn't liked the man to begin with.)

It turned out that the substitute wasn't just mean to his students; he was rude to everyone. He cursed out people who drove too fast or too slow. He insulted the cashier at the drive-through espresso stand. He even said nasty things to the people on the car radio, who Fuzzy was pretty sure couldn't hear him.

Clapping his paws over his ears, Fuzzy gritted his teeth. He faced a dilemma. How could he learn the sub's weaknesses if he couldn't stand to listen to him?

After an annoying car ride, Mr. Brittle hefted the messenger bag again. *Schoomp! Beep-beep!* The door slammed and an alarm chirped. Fuzzy clung to a textbook as the satchel swung back and forth. Up some stairs and down an echoey hall they went.

The faint sounds of a flute and piano played somewhere nearby. Soothing stuff, Fuzzy thought. *Bam-bam-bam!* A fist pounded on a door.

"Turn that awful music down!" yelled Mr. Brittle. "How many times must I tell you?"

Fuzzy couldn't make out the neighbor's shouted reply, but in another few seconds, he heard the music crank up several notches. The teacher swore, banged on the door again, and shouted, "You just wait—I will take this to the condo board, do you hear?"

Clearly, thought Fuzzy, Mr. Brittle was the ambassador of aloha for his condominium.

When the man got no further reply from his neighbor, he grumbled to himself and moved on. Unlocking a nearby door, he opened it and went inside. Keys clinked as they dropped into a bowl. With a heavy thump, the messenger bag landed on a hard surface. Footsteps retreated. Running water burbled from another room.

Cautiously, Fuzzy crawled to the mouth of the bag and sniffed. A piney scent greeted him, along with a faint, musky odor that made him vaguely uneasy. Of course, who was he kidding? Just being inside Mr. Brittle's apartment made Fuzzy uneasy.

He poked his head out of the satchel and found it was resting on a low table near an angular gray couch that looked as soft and comfortable as a block of concrete. Fuzzy crept out a little farther, scanning in all directions. The room was empty.

The sparsely decorated space displayed all the charm and warmth of a prison cell in January. No pictures hung on the walls; no color brightened the room. All was gray, black, and brown.

Stepping out onto the table, Fuzzy cast about for clues to this strange man's inner workings. No magazines cluttered the tabletop, just a single thick book: *Crime and Punishment*.

No wonder he's such a cheerful guy, thought Fuzzy.

A clatter from the next room reminded him that his position was completely exposed. When a lean figure crossed the nearest doorway, Fuzzy held stock-still. Had he been noticed? Mr. Brittle headed deeper into the apartment, and Fuzzy let out a long breath.

Clearly, he couldn't stay on the table. His best move was to find somewhere to hide until the teacher went to sleep, then search around for clues.

Footfalls sounded, drawing closer.

Fuzzy leaped off the coffee table and darted under the couch. Just in time. The feet clomped their way up to the table, turned around, and planted themselves directly in front of Fuzzy. The sofa bottom sagged above him.

One by one, Mr. Brittle unlaced his shoes and took them off. A smell like moldy cheese and rotten broccoli wafted out.

Fuzzy fanned the air. *Whew.* How did humans get so stinky? Maybe from all the weird food they ate. Deep-fried potato slices? Waffles? It was a wonder they could survive.

Settling in, Fuzzy tried to breathe through his mouth. It helped, a little.

The feet shifted. The thump of a book and the rustle of paper told Fuzzy that Mr. Brittle was pulling things from his messenger bag. Fuzzy blew out a sigh of relief. Good thing he wasn't still inside it!

The television clicked on. For a while, Fuzzy listened to newscasters yammer while the teacher did things with books and paper above him. He fidgeted. It seemed like he might be in for a long, boring wait. How could he entertain himself?

Clearly not with the news program. Fuzzy scanned under the couch for something to help pass the time. He found the crust from an old sandwich, paper clips, lint balls the size of his head, a stray sock, small change, three Froot Loops, and an irritable spider. Fuzzy tried nibbling one of the cereal bits, but it had about as much flavor as the lint ball.

Beedle-deedle-dee. Mr. Brittle's cell phone chirped. "What?" said the teacher.

"Is this Mr. Brittle?" asked a chipper voice from the phone's speaker. "*Chad* Brittle?"

The sub muted the TV. "Yes?" he said warily.

"I'm Sonya Starr from Hot Pop Entertainment," burbled the phone voice. "We've got an exciting proposal for you."

Fuzzy cocked his head to listen. *Mr. Brittle* and *exciting* were not words you'd normally put together.

"What is this all about?" said the sub. He'd gone beyond wary to downright suspicious. "Are you trying to sell me a magazine subscription?"

"A reality TV show!" Sonya bubbled, like she was

discussing a delicious tray of fresh parsley. "We're assembling four teams of former boy-band members to—"

"Stop right there," said Mr. Brittle. "Those days are over. I do not play music anymore."

Fuzzy's jaw dropped. The Meanest Sub in the Universe used to be in a boy band? He used to actually *like* music? Fuzzy couldn't have been more surprised if a wildebeest Michael Jackson impersonator had moonwalked out of the kitchen.

"Oh, but we've got coaches to help get you—" Sonya Starr began.

"No," said Mr. Brittle.

"And you'll be living in a mansion while we film the—"

"*No!*" yelled the sub. "No, no, no! Are you deaf? Am I speaking Swahili? I will not do it."

"But we already—" The woman's voice cut out, midsentence.

Fuzzy's head whirled like a hamster wheel. He'd seen quite a lot of TV at Miss Wills's house, and he knew that boy bands were all about the big smiles and fancy haircuts and slick moves. He couldn't picture Mr. Brittle smiling, let alone singing and dancing.

Above him, the sub gave a frustrated growl. The feet in their gray socks left the couch and began to pace. When the cell phone rang again, he ignored it.

"Let us get the band back together," Mr. Brittle said in a mocking voice. "It will be so much fun, like having all your teeth pulled." He continued pacing, muttering phrases like "big mistake," "laughing at me," and "never again."

Questions chased one another around Fuzzy's mind like puppies on a playdate. What had happened to turn Mr. Brittle from a teen idol to a terror? Why wouldn't he listen to music anymore? And most important of all, was this information something that the pets could use to drive him off?

He put his chin on his paws and thought deep thoughts. But before he knew it, Fuzzy fell asleep without any answers.

CHAPTER 11

A Bobo No-No

When Fuzzy awoke, the room was dim and something was growling. He tensed, checking for predators, until he realized that the growling was coming from his own stomach.

Fuzzy was hungry.

He sniffed. The stinky sock odor had faded. The apartment was quiet. Maybe Mr. Brittle had gone to sleep?

Ever so cautiously, he edged out from beneath

the sofa. The room was dark, lit only by moonlight through the windows. Snores rumbled from somewhere to the right, so Fuzzy turned left, following his nose toward the source of faint food smells.

Another whiff of that unsettling musky odor drifted past, but since Fuzzy couldn't place it, he kept heading for the kitchen. A guinea pig has priorities, after all. And satisfying hunger was right up at the top of the list.

Fuzzy's trusty nose led him off the carpet into another room. And just as he rounded the corner, Fuzzy slammed into a furry creature as slim and evil-looking as Mr. Brittle himself.

"Gah!" Fuzzy staggered back in shock. His belly gave a flip. "Wh-who are you?"

Reeling from their collision, the ferret swayed and twisted to regain its balance. Two black eyes in a dark mask locked on to Fuzzy. That musky scent he'd detected earlier was now strong enough to outwrestle an anaconda.

"Intruder!" the creature screamed, clutching its paws to its chest.

"No, I, uh—" Fuzzy began. He reached out.

The ferret hissed, recoiling. "Stranger danger!"

"I—I mean you no harm," said Fuzzy, whose own heart was thudding faster than a flamenco dancer's heels. "I'm a guinea pig from Mr.—"

The creature's eyes widened. "Guinea pig?" It sniffed curiously. "That means you . . . are prey. Bobo likes prey."

Fuzzy didn't like the look in Bobo's eyes. Raising his palms, he began backing away across the living room. "No, *not* prey! I'm a, uh, visitor from your owner's classroom."

Bobo stalked forward, his gaze drilling into Fuzzy. "Master never brings me prey, but Bobo is a good hunter. Bobo will show Master."

Casting about for something to distract the ferret, Fuzzy spotted a red rubber ball beneath a high table. He angled toward it, saying, "Hey, what's the deal with your master, anyway? Why does he act so mean to everyone?"

Still advancing, Bobo shook his head. "Master is not mean. Master pets Bobo, Master feeds Bobo, Master is the best."

"Are we talking about the same master?" Fuzzy had a hard time picturing Mr. Brittle taking care of a goldfish, to say nothing of a pet like the ferret.

"Master is always good," said Bobo. His eyes gleamed with a true-believer light that originated from someplace between Creepy Town and Nuttsburg.

Fuzzy groped behind him and touched the cool rubber surface. "Tell me."

"What?"

"Does your master like to play . . . ball?" In a flash, he turned, seized the orb, and flung it into the living room.

"Ball!" cried Bobo, wheeling in pursuit.

As soon as the ferret's attention left him, Fuzzy turned and fled. He dashed out of the living room and into a smaller space that looked like an office.

"Tricky guinea pig!" cried the ferret. "Bobo will find you."

Holy haystacks! Fuzzy needed a place to hide from this nutjob, and quick. He didn't know if the ferret's comment about *prey* was kidding or serious, and he really didn't want to find out.

Urgently, he scanned the room. It held the usual office stuff: a desk and chair, a bookcase, a computer stand and wastebasket. The ferret was taller and stronger than he was; where could Fuzzy possibly hide?

"I'm *co*-ming!" Bobo singsonged.

Chills rolled along Fuzzy's spine like ice-cold pill bugs tobogganing down a hill. He cast about for sanctuary.

In the corner, a sliding door stood ajar!

Fresh out of options, Fuzzy sprinted over, slipped inside, and, shoving with all his might, narrowed the gap to a mere crack. The smell of cedar and mothballs assaulted his nose, but he paid it no mind. Fuzzy put an eye to the crack.

In the spill of moonlight through the window, a lanky silhouette crept into the office.

"Hide and seeeek," crooned the ferret. "Bobo's favorite game."

He sniffed the air, drifting toward the desk. "Let's see. Is guinea pig behind the . . . *wastebasket?*" The ferret pounced, upending the trash bin. "Is it in the . . . *bookcase?*" Again the creature lunged, knocking some DVDs off a low shelf.

Fuzzy's insides flip-flopped like a circus acrobat; his paws trembled. Very soon, this loony ferret would run out of places to look, and then he'd check the closet.

Fuzzy glanced around him. Nothing but boxes and shoes, and hanging above, a rack of overcoats. Nowhere to hide.

He put his shoulder to the door and slid it all the way closed. Then he planted his feet and braced himself against the door's metal frame.

Bobo's voice sounded nearer. "I wonder, oh, I wonder, where that piggy could be? Is it in the . . . *closet*?" At that, something thumped into the door from the other side. It pressed against his shoulder.

Fuzzy's heart gave a hitch. He crouched lower, digging his claws into the nubbly carpet for traction. As soon as Bobo figured out that the door slid open rather than pushed, Fuzzy was in deep, deep doo-doo.

"Aha!" cried the ferret. "Little piggy, if you don't let Bobo in, he's going to huff and puff and—*hyeeeugh* your house down!" Bobo heaved again, harder.

A long pause. Fuzzy could almost feel the ferret's mind working.

"O-ho!" said Bobo. "The door goes slidey-slide, not pushy-push." Claws scrabbled on the metal frame, inches away from Fuzzy's shoulder. *Hyeeeugh!"*

The door jerked open an inch. Fuzzy felt his feet slip. He frantically shoved the slider closed.

It was only a matter of time before that masked maniac would out-shove him. Still, Fuzzy swore to resist until his final breath. He tensed for another assault and then . . .

Bright light flooded through the narrow crack beneath the door.

"What the hey?" It was Mr. Brittle. "Bobo, you naughty, naughty boy. How did you get out of your cage?"

"Master, there's an intruder!" cried the ferret. "Bobo hunted him down."

The teacher's voice sounded very close to the door. "You know you should only come out when I am watching, you little troublemaker. Right back into the cage with you, widdle Bo-Biddle."

Bo-Biddle? thought Fuzzy. *Sweet name for a psycho.*

Even so, he couldn't believe how tender the man sounded. Almost as if he had a heart.

The ferret begged his master to set him down, but it seemed that Mr. Brittle could no more understand ferret talk than Fuzzy could manage to pole-vault. Their voices receded, and the lights went out.

Fuzzy waited. He wanted to be absolutely positive that the teacher was asleep and the ferret behind bars before venturing out again. Easing open the sliding door until moonlight penetrated the closet, he decided to kill time by snooping.

The nearest box was already open. Fuzzy clambered up inside and rummaged around. It seemed to contain lots of photos and clippings, as well as some plaques that might have been awards.

He held up one of the photos, angled it into the light, and peered at it closely. When he recognized the face, Fuzzy snorted in surprise.

It was a big, glossy image of a young man's face, much like the autographed photos of authors and actors that hung in Miss Wills's den at her home. The eyes smoldered like burnt toast, the hair hung long and floppy, and the thin lips were twisted into a pouty smile.

But it was a younger Mr. Brittle, all the same.

The photo was autographed:

Badd Boyz 4 Eva!
All my love, Chad

Fuzzy couldn't help it—he *wheek*ed softly in amazement. He shook his head wonderingly.

Just wait until the other pets got a load of this!

CHAPTER 12

Fuzzy Takes Flight

Fuzzy awoke with a snort to find himself huddled under Mr. Brittle's photo. He yawned. Morning light streamed in through the office window, penetrating the closet and hurting his eyes.

Morning?!

He leaped to his feet. Had Mr. Brittle left for school yet? Was Fuzzy stranded in the sub's apartment with only a deranged ferret for company?

He poked his head out of the closet door and listened. A clattering came from another room, along with the mutter of voices. Either Mr. Brittle had a visitor, or he was watching TV again. The bitter tang of coffee drifted in the air.

Fuzzy relaxed. He hadn't overslept after all. But now he faced a different challenge: How would he sneak back into the teacher's messenger bag without being detected?

He squeezed through the narrow gap and into the office, scanning for danger. No ferret, no Mr. Brittle. So far, so good. Soundlessly, Fuzzy crept across the carpet to the office doorway. He peeked around the edge . . .

And ducked back as the sub stepped into the living room wearing sky-blue pajamas and carrying a smallish paper sack. Fuzzy pressed his back to the wall, heart hammering.

Had he been spotted? Should he take cover?

Fuzzy listened intently as Mr. Brittle's heavy footsteps receded. He let out a long breath. After another minute, he risked a quick glance. The coast was clear.

Fuzzy readied himself for the dash, and then a sudden thought stopped him in his tracks. His eyes were drawn back to the closet. For a few seconds, he wavered. Then, before he could change his mind, Fuzzy dashed back to where he'd spent the night, snatched Mr. Brittle's teen idol photo, and hustled back to the office doorway.

He checked left, right. Then Fuzzy gathered his courage and raced across the living room floor, photo flapping behind him. Just before he reached the coffee table, a familiar voice froze him in his tracks.

"Fee, fi, fo, fum, I smell the smell of a piggy . . . um."

It was Bobo. The ferret might not have been much of a poet, but he had a keen sniffer.

Fuzzy whirled. On the far side of the living room, Bobo was slinking through the doorway like Dracula's shadow. His eyes sparkled with jolly insanity.

Suffering mange mites! Fuzzy flung the photo on top of the ottoman and scrambled up after it. His heart felt like it was about to thump right through his chest.

"I'm coming for yooou," crooned the ferret. He stalked forward as Fuzzy trembled.

Fuzzy's natural guinea pig instinct was to freeze in place until the danger went away. But this danger was drawing ever closer.

He risked a glance at the coffee table. The teacher's satchel was so near, resting beside the brown paper bag. But almost a foot's distance separated the table from his perch.

Too far to jump . . .

Taking a step back, Fuzzy felt the photograph crinkle under his foot.

. . . Or was it?

A mad idea popped into his head. The ferret was slinking closer, humming an evil ferret tune. Fuzzy would get only one chance at this. He fought his instincts and won.

He reached down, picked up the oversized photo, and held it above his head with both paws, arms spread wide. He retreated as far back as he could go, gritted his teeth, and ran like lightning, leaping straight off the edge of the ottoman.

Time seemed to slow.

Fuzzy felt the slight tug as the photo caught a draft. He glimpsed Bobo's upturned face beneath him, gaping upward. And he saw the table ahead, drawing closer, closer . . .

Time sped back up with a *whoomp* as his hind feet caught the edge of the table, and Fuzzy tumbled like an acrobat, over and over.

Thoonk. He collided with the satchel and finally stopped. When Fuzzy raised his head, both he and the photo were safe on the tabletop.

"Not fair!" cried Bobo. "Guinea pigs can't fly!"

Still a bit dizzy, Fuzzy climbed to his feet. He had to think fast. The ferret would be upon him before he could hide, and Mr. Brittle might come through the door at any moment.

"Guinea pig is tricky," said Bobo from below. "But nothing stops Bobo."

Fuzzy scanned the table for anything that could distract the ferret. All he saw was the satchel, the sack lunch, and the photo.

The photo?

In a flash of inspiration, he picked it up and held it before him, leaning over the edge of the table, so that the image of the teen idol faced the ferret.

"Widdle Bo-Biddle is a very naughty boy," said Fuzzy, in his best Mr. Brittle imitation.

"Master?" came the ferret's voice.

"Bobo should go back to his cage right now!"

"I, uh," the ferret stammered. "But . . ."

Fuzzy ducked back out of sight. Quickly, while his opponent was still confused, he folded the picture in half and scrambled up inside the messenger bag, then hid under the photo like a tent.

And not a second too soon.

"Bobo?" came the teacher's voice. "*There* you are. Back in the cage, you widdle rascal. No arguments."

"Master?" said Bobo, sounding thoroughly confused. "But how . . . ?"

Their voices receded as Mr. Brittle carried his pet away.

Fuzzy exhaled a sigh of relief gustier than a giant's sneeze. Worn out by his morning adventure, he curled up under his improvised shelter and dropped into a light doze. Even the satchel swaying as Mr. Brittle headed off to work barely roused him.

His last thought as he drifted off was, *Thank Darwin for dumb ferrets.*

CHAPTER 13

Idol Threats

When Mr. Brittle learned of the all-school safety assembly that morning, he groused and grumbled. "A waste of time!" he muttered. But since every class was going, he finally relented, leading the students out the door.

As soon as they'd gone, Fuzzy seized his chance. Quick as a flash, he escaped his cage and scampered off to call an emergency meeting of the Class Pets Club. He wanted to share his news—but more than that, they had to put a stop to the sour substitute before it was too late.

"You *what*?" squawked Sassafras after Fuzzy had begun his story. "Get out of town!"

The rest of the pets crowded around Fuzzy in their clubhouse, listening to his tale and marveling at the photo of young Mr. Brittle.

"And you should have seen that Bobo," said Fuzzy. "He was nuttier than a squirrel's sundae."

Cinnabun looked around at the rest of the pets. "Well, hush my mouth. He faced a ferret and lived to tell about it. And he went above and beyond the call, all for the good of his students. I think Brother Fuzzy deserves special recognition."

"What did you have in mind?" asked Marta.

"Ooh, let's sing him the Freeze Song," Mistletoe suggested.

Igor arched his brow. "The Freeze Song?"

"You know," said Mistletoe, picking up the melody. "Freeze a jolly good fellow, freeze a jolly good fellow . . ."

The other pets joined in, belting out the lyrics with gusto. Fuzzy ducked his head, feeling his cheeks go warm.

When they finished, Cinnabun patted him on the shoulder. "Well done, Brother Fuzzy."

"So your Mr. Brittle was really in a boy band?" said Luther. "Crazy, baby."

"It's true," said Fuzzy. "According to the stuff in those boxes, they made two albums. The Badd Boyz were on TV and everything."

"Wowza-yowza," breathed Mistletoe.

"Holy heartthrob!" said the parakeet. "So the Meanest Sub in the Universe used to be a teen idol?"

Cinnabun cocked her head wistfully. "He must really miss the music."

Glancing up from his fruit chew, Igor snorted. "He's got a funny way of showing it."

"Look, him being in a boy band is weird, I admit," said Fuzzy, "but there's a more important question."

"Who put the bomp in the wop-bop-a-lu-bomp?" said Igor.

"No—how can we use this to help make him leave?"

The other pets offered frowns and shrugs. For a while, nobody said anything. All that could be heard was the hum of some machine deep inside the school building and the sound of an iguana munching a snack.

"Maybe if we play music he hates really, really loudly, he'll run away?" said Mistletoe.

"His neighbor already does that," said Fuzzy.

"And?" asked the mouse.

"No luck so far."

Mistletoe slumped, toying with some loose threads on her pillow.

Marta stared thoughtfully into the candle flame. "Fuzzy, you said Mr. Brittle got an offer to rejoin the band and be on TV again?"

"Yeah," said Fuzzy. "He turned it down flat."

The tortoise's kind eyes crinkled in a smile. "What if we could somehow convince him to take it?"

Fuzzy met her gaze. A faint tingle danced down his limbs. It might have been fur mites, but he thought it was hope.

"After all," Marta continued, "that would solve both his problem and ours."

"*His* problem?" Luther uncoiled lazily. "I thought his problem was that he's a miserable excuse for a human being."

Marta shook her head. "Not really. I think he turned mean because he's so disappointed."

"That's totally whackadoodle," said Sassafras. "Wouldn't someone who's disappointed act sad?"

"Who knows?" said Igor. "Humans are weird."

Cinnabun licked her shoulder, grooming herself. "Sister Marta's right. That man gave up everything he loved because—um, why did he give it up, Brother Fuzzy?"

Fuzzy scratched himself. "From the magazine clipping I saw, it looks like everyone loved the band's first album. Then Badd Boyz made a second album that stank. Critics panned it, and the band broke up."

"So our Mr. Brittle didn't quit music by choice," said the bunny. "My stars, that would make anyone sadder than a slice of stale carrot cake."

"Yeah, but if he was any good, why not just start a new group?" Igor broke off a piece of fruit chew, tossed it into the air, and caught it in his mouth.

Fuzzy thought about the beginning of the school year. Back then he'd tried to become Class Pets president but had been beaten by Cinnabun. "Maybe he lost confidence," he said quietly.

"My thought exactly," said the bunny. "So he gave up, and it turned him bitter, poor thing."

"Poor thing?" said Fuzzy. "He's bullying my kids and making them miserable. *They're* the poor things."

"True," said the bunny. "But doesn't that unfortunate man also deserve our pity?"

"No way!" cried Fuzzy, Luther, Sassafras, and Igor.

Marta and Cinnabun exchanged a look. "Maybe if he got a little more sympathy," said the tortoise, "he might be a little less mean."

"Amen, sister!" said Cinnabun.

Fuzzy lifted an eyebrow. "You think that showing him the milk of rodent kindness will change him? I've got news for you: Mr. Brittle is bad to the bone."

"Amen, brother!" Igor smirked.

"Besides," Fuzzy said, massaging his forehead, "none of this is getting us any closer to a plan."

Cinnabun nibbled on one of her front claws. Marta stared into space. Luther uncoiled one way, then coiled up the other.

"I've got an idea," squeaked Mistletoe.

Everyone turned with a start. She'd been so quiet, Fuzzy had forgotten she was there.

"*Ssso?*" hissed Luther. "Lay it on us, little bit."

Clearing her throat, Mistletoe glanced around at the others. "Well, I was thinking . . . if music got him into this mess, maybe music could get us out of it."

"Pinch me," Igor told Fuzzy. "I think the mouse is finally making sense."

Fuzzy pinched him.

"Ow!" said the iguana. "Don't be so literal."

Leaning forward, Cinnabun asked Mistletoe, "Do you have an actual plan, sweet girl?"

"We just have to remind him how much fun it is to sing and dance," said the mouse. "Right?"

Fuzzy's brow furrowed. "It couldn't be that easy," he said. "Could it?"

"Why not?" asked Mistletoe.

"Well . . ." Fuzzy bit his lip. "Maybe. I guess if Mr. Brittle remembers how fun it is to perform, he might want to give up being a teacher."

"Which he's terrible at anyway," said Igor.

"But here's the problem," said Fuzzy. "He's probably seen *some* singing and dancing over the past ten years, and he hasn't quit teaching yet."

"It'd have to be something really different," said Marta. "Something special."

Sassafras's eyes opened wide. "Ooh! I know! One of us should sing and dance for him. That'd be special."

Luther rolled his eyes.

"He'll be so inspired," said the parakeet, "he won't be able to help himself."

"Inspired to lose his lunch," muttered Igor.

Clapping her paws together, Cinnabun cried, "Bless your heart, Sister Sassafras! That's a splendid idea." She knuckled her dimple in typically adorable fashion. "But however shall we pick the performer?"

Fuzzy raised a skeptical eyebrow. Two to one odds, she was angling to do it herself.

"The only fair way would be to hold auditions," said Marta, "just like the students do for the school play."

"Fun-*tastic!*" squeaked Mistletoe, eyes shining. "And we can all vote for our favorite, like the judges on those TV shows."

"Sweet fancy Moses on buttered toast!" cried Cinnabun. "We're holding auditions!"

"Yay!" cheered Sassafras and Mistletoe.

Fuzzy hated to mention it; still, he felt he had to. "But if one of us does this, won't it blow our cover? Mr. Brittle will realize that that pet isn't just an ordinary pet."

"Nah, he'll think someone trained us to do it," said Sassafras. "Humans only see what they want to see."

"Well, if you're sure . . ." said Fuzzy.

Cinnabun nodded definitively. "It's well worth the risk. Now, everyone who wants to try out, take a few minutes to work up a routine. Then we'll let you strut your stuff."

The pets scattered to figure out their dance steps.

"Ooh," said Sassafras. "I'm doing something by Lady GooGoo."

"Pretty sure that's Gaga," said Luther.

"GooGoo, Gaga, either way, I'll be a hit!" The parakeet fluttered off to one side of the clubhouse and began practicing her moves.

Fuzzy glanced at Igor, who was sitting back on his pillow.

"Don't look at me," said the iguana. "I'm strictly a judge."

Blowing out a sigh, Fuzzy retreated to his own corner. He wasn't what you'd call a Dancing Rodent, but if it meant getting rid of the Evil Sub, he was willing to try anything. Feeling a total fool, he attempted a few steps. He didn't actually trip over his own feet, but that was about the best you could say for his dancing.

All too soon, Cinnabun called the pets together and formed them into a circle. Wearing a huge grin, she met their gazes, one by one.

"Okay, Class Pets, so you think you can dance?" said the bunny. "Come on up and show us how!"

And just like that, auditions began.

CHAPTER 14

The "Ick" Factor

Enthusiasm goes a long way. But it doesn't go *all* the way. Some actual talent is required.

As Fuzzy watched the other pets perform, he thought that somehow their auditions weren't quite in the same league as those song and dance competitions he'd seen on TV. Instead of colored lights and a killer sound system, they had a few votive candles and a handful of animals humming along in different keys. Instead of slick steps and flawless singing, they had . . .

Luther wiggling a half-baked hula to some half-remembered Hawaiian song.

Cinnabun performing a hip-hop anthem with ten times the hopping (and half the hipness) of the original.

And Sassafras belting out a Broadway show tune that sounded like someone had tossed *The Sound of Music* into a blender and hit liquefy. For her big finale, she flew round and round the clubhouse until her wings put out all the candles, causing her to fly into

Cinnabun, knock the president off her podium, and squash the grapes.

Fuzzy tried to be upbeat. But he just didn't see how any of this qualified as special—at least not in a good way. He couldn't picture Mr. Brittle saying, "I'm going back into show business now!" after watching one of the pets perform.

But how could he mention this, when his fellow pets were trying so hard to help out? It seemed almost criminal to crush their enthusiasm.

Fuzzy joined the others in applauding Mistletoe's tap dance, while privately wondering whether they'd overlooked some other way to motivate Mr. Brittle. When all the pets who wanted to audition had finished and everyone had sat down, the club took a vote.

None of the wannabe performers got more than two nods. Most received only one vote: their own.

After tallying things up, Cinnabun winced. "We've got a two-way tie, y'all. No matter how many times we vote, it keeps ending up the same."

Mistletoe wrinkled her nose. "So what does that mean?"

"It means there's no clear winner," said the bunny.

"And what does *that* mean?" asked Mistletoe.

With a shrug, Cinnabun said, "We're deadlocked."

The pets avoided one another's eyes. "So nobody gets to sing and dance for the guy?" asked the mouse.

"Nobody," said Luther.

A smile tugged at Fuzzy's lips as an idea struck him. "Or maybe *every*body," he said.

Luther frowned. "*Sss*ay what?"

"If none of us is good enough on our own," Fuzzy said, "maybe it'll take all of us together to make a big impression."

Mistletoe's face lit up like a Christmas tree. "Abso-tutely!" she cried. "He'd never be able to forget that."

Fuzzy agreed wholeheartedly. Whether the club's performance was good-memorable or bad-memorable, it would definitely capture Mr. Brittle's attention. Although whether that would be enough to thrust him out of teaching and back into show business, Fuzzy couldn't say.

"You realize that if all of us dance," said Luther, "we're exposing what we can do, big-time."

Fuzzy nibbled on his whiskers. "It's a gamble, all right. Is everyone up for it?"

"Yes!" the other pets responded.

"All righty then," said Luther. "Let's get to it."

Still, before they could put their talents to the test, a small host of problems had to be solved. Starting with . . .

"If we're going to dance, who will teach us the steps?" asked Marta. "I'm not really a hot-footed hoofer."

"None of us are," said Fuzzy.

"Speak for yourself, Brother Fuzzy." Cinnabun sniffed. "Personally, I've spent hours watching *Celebrity Dance-Off* at Miss Nakamura's house. I know all the moves and then some."

"Then I nominate Cinnabun to be our corey-ogg—

our, um, chore-hog. Umm . . ." Mistletoe fumbled for the word.

"Teacher of dance steps?" suggested Fuzzy.

"Pre-zactly!" said Mistletoe.

"And I'll help!" Sassafras crowed. "I've got Broadway in my bones!"

"And feathers in your brain," muttered Igor.

The parakeet scowled. "At least that's better than rocks."

Before the two pets could resume their usual squabbling, Cinnabun stepped in. "Thanks, y'all. I'd be tickled pink to serve as our choreographer. Let's start by having all the boys stand over here and all the girls over there." She wrangled the pets into two lines.

Igor slouched apart from the rest with arms crossed.

"Why don't you join us, Brother Igor?" asked Cinnabun.

"As I mentioned earlier," said the iguana, "I don't dance."

Sassafras flapped a wing. "Nonsense. Everyone can dance. It's just walking set to music."

Igor scowled. "I didn't say I *can't* dance; I said I don't."

"What's the difference?" asked Mistletoe.

"Attitude," said Luther.

Igor lifted his chin. "We iguanas have an image to maintain. Dancing around like a fool doesn't fit into that image."

"But *standing* around like a fool does?" teased Sassafras.

Before he could retort, Cinnabun put a paw on his shoulder. "Please dance with us," she pleaded. "It won't be the same without you."

"Pretty pretty please?" added Mistletoe.

The iguana shook his head. "My mind is made up."

A sly expression crept across Luther's face. It looked very natural there. "Aw, don't pressure him," said the snake. "He's just afraid."

"Who's afraid?" Igor bristled.

The boa shrugged, making his coils ripple. "No shame, baby. It's perfectly natural to feel fear."

"I'm not afraid of anything," said Igor.

Luther continued as if he hadn't heard. "When you're not as talented as others, of course you'd be afraid to perform. No one likes to look bad."

The iguana's back spines got spikier. "Who said that? Who said I'm not as talented?"

Keeping his attention focused on Cinnabun and Mistletoe, Luther went on, "So really, the polite thing would be to stop pressuring Igor. He's dealing with enough already."

Elbowing his way between them, the iguana lifted his front feet. "Hold it right there. For the sake of our club's reputation, I can see I'll have to join in and show you all how it's done."

Smothering a smile, Cinnabun said, "Oh, well, if you're sure it won't be too much trouble . . ."

"No sacrifice too great for the club," Igor said gruffly.

Fuzzy felt a rush of optimism. He didn't know if

one pet made a difference in this crazy scheme, but he was glad that the whole club stood together. Maybe there was strength in numbers.

"Can we perform this dance for Mr. Brittle today, after school?" he asked.

"Why today?" said Sassafras.

"He always stays late," said Fuzzy, "and that would be the perfect opportunity."

Cinnabun clapped her paws together. "Let's shake a leg, y'all!" she cried. "We've got a lot of steps to learn if we're going to help those kids. The sooner we learn, the sooner we can blow Mr. Brittle's mind." She began teaching their first moves.

And the sooner we blow his mind, the less damage he'll inflict on my students, thought Fuzzy, stumbling his way through a box step.

Their plan would work.

It had to—they were taking a risk that might expose them for good. And they all knew they wouldn't get a second chance.

CHAPTER 15

Brittle Go Peep

Over and over, the pets drilled their choreography until their legs were rubbery and their feet (or in Luther's case, his belly) were sore. At last, exhausted, they dragged themselves back to their own cages to rest. The pets weren't ready, but that didn't really matter.

Ready or not, their show must go on—Fuzzy knew the students couldn't stand another week of Mr. Brittle's bullying.

With Miss Wills's speedy return still seeming as likely as a unicorn ride through Central Park, the students of 5-B were losing all hope. Gone were the lively debates on American history, the before-school babble of excitement about learning, the fun-loving attitudes. The kids took Mr. Brittle's insults stoically and silently.

Nervous Lily spent the afternoon with her head down on her desk, responding only when the sub asked her a direct question. Loud Brandon stopped talking entirely. Spiky Diego, Fuzzy noticed, hadn't even come to school.

Another week of this treatment, and there would be no class for Miss Wills to return to—or at least, not one that she would recognize. Assuming Mr. Brittle didn't manage to replace her first.

Fuzzy shivered. That future was just too awful to contemplate.

The time was now. By hook or by crook, the pets were going to get rid of the Meanest Sub in the Universe before the sun set, even if Fuzzy had to give him a case of rabies to make that happen. (Not that he knew how to catch rabies, but it was the thought that counted.)

He suffered through that afternoon with gritted teeth. No read-aloud, no creative writing, no artistic expression of any kind for the kids—just deadly dull lectures and boring exercises. What was the point of school, Fuzzy wondered, if it didn't awaken your imagination?

But apparently certain humans didn't share a guinea pig's opinions on education.

The hours limped on. You might think that, with the kids offering no opposition, Mr. Brittle would ease up on the bullying. If so, you don't know bullies. The sub's mean remarks and petty punishments went on and on. It was like the lack of resistance encouraged him to push his cruelties even further, out to the very limits.

Fuzzy longed for Miss Wills's comforting snuggles and was yearning to spend the weekend with her, far away from Mr. Brittle. But then he thought, *What if that meanie won't even let me go home with her?* His emotions were a stew of anxiety and worry, spiced with outrage.

By the last minutes of class, Fuzzy was champing at the bit. Would the school day never end? Finally, he watched the students trudge out the door, and the substitute tackled his after-school paperwork. Up and down his cage Fuzzy paced, waiting for Sassafras to make her move.

For their plan to succeed, they'd need split-second timing. But since the pets weren't much on timing, Fuzzy knew that in the end, it would all come down to dumb luck.

He only hoped their luck was dumb enough.

Just when Fuzzy was about to jump out of his skin, he heard the crackle of the intercom—or, to be more accurate, Sassafras imitating the intercom.

"Paging Mr. Brittle," said the bird, mimicking the principal's voice. "Principal Flake calling."

"Uh, yes," said the sub, frowning curiously. "I am here."

Fuzzy noticed him checking around for the intercom switch. Hopefully, the man wouldn't figure out that the real loudspeaker wasn't a two-way system, and that Sassafras was hiding in the crawl space just above it.

"That's excellent, just excellent," said Sassafras-as-Flake. "Mr. Brittle, I need you to attend a meeting now."

The sub rolled his eyes. "Can it wait until Monday? I am busy."

"No!" squawked the bird. Mr. Brittle shot the loudspeaker a sharp look. "I mean, um, no, this can't wait. It's a very, very important meeting, full of vital . . . importance."

"Can one of the other teachers . . . ?"

"Nope, this is a super-duper special private meeting," said Sassafras. "Just you and me. Top secret."

Fuzzy bit his lip. The parakeet was getting carried away; would Mr. Brittle suspect something?

"Just me, huh?" said the substitute. "Where . . . ?"

"The music room," said Sassafras. "Ten minutes."

"The *music* room?!" Mr. Brittle protested.

But with one last crackle, the bird fell silent.

"Huh," the sub muttered. "Wonder what that old bat wants?"

That old bat is actually an old bird, Fuzzy reflected. He felt glad the man didn't know how close to the mark he'd come. As quietly as possible, Fuzzy began rearranging his blocks and ball, preparing to make his escape.

Mr. Brittle worked a little while longer, then glanced at the clock and packed away his papers and books. Fuzzy sat up as the teacher passed him, heading for the door.

"Bye-bye, piggy!" said Mr. Brittle. "With any luck, I will soon replace your teacher. And then, I will bring my own sweet Bobo in here and replace *you* too."

Fuzzy gasped. His suspicions were true! But he couldn't let that awful sub know he'd gotten under Fuzzy's skin.

"With any luck, you'll quit tomorrow, and we'll all throw a party!" said Fuzzy defiantly. Still, he knew it would take more than luck to drive that man from his classroom.

It would take a miracle.

The instant the door thumped closed, Fuzzy scrambled up his makeshift steps and over the cage wall. He set a new speedy-escape record, hurtling over the cubbyholes and hustling up the bookcase. Fuzzy hoped against hope that the custodian and any late-staying staff weren't feeling too observant, because all the class pets would be out of their cages and running free.

Kicking up dust, he galloped along through the crawl space, lickety-split. Fuzzy shaved some time off his trek by using a shortcut across a block of classrooms, rather than taking the long way around like Mr. Brittle. In fact, he got going so fast, he wasn't sure exactly where he was.

Skidding to a halt, Fuzzy lifted a ceiling tile to check his whereabouts. Below him yawned the empty corridor outside the computer room. Wiggling whiskers—he'd overshot his target!

Fuzzy was about to drop the tile back into place when he saw a familiar head of hair atop a familiar body bobbing up the hallway. Blonde highlights, gray roots, and enough hairspray that not even a follicle quivered.

Mrs. Flake, the principal. And her path would take her right past the music room.

Uh-oh.

What would happen if she bumped into Mr. Brittle before he entered the chamber where all the pets were waiting?

Disaster, that was what.

Fuzzy did the only thing he could think of. Sucking in a huge breath, he *wheek-wheek*ed at the top of his lungs, shouting, "Hey, Mrs. Flake!"

The principal whirled, scanning right and left but seeing nothing.

"Up here!" he squeaked.

Mrs. Flake's head snapped back, and Fuzzy found himself eye to eye with the most powerful person at Leo Gumpus Elementary.

The woman gasped. She pulled a walkie-talkie from her belt and barked into it, "Mr. Poole, come in, please?"

"Go ahead, Mrs. F," came the custodian's warm voice.

"Guinea pig at twelve o'clock!"

A brief silence. "Um, but it's not even four yet."

The principal gave a wordless growl. "Twelve o'clock! Right above me—there's a guinea pig peeking through the ceiling."

"Oh. Why didn't you say so?"

Mrs. Flake just shook her head in response.

"Tell me where you are and I'll come rescue Fuzzy," said Mr. Darius.

"West corridor, just outside the computer room." The principal peered up at Fuzzy. "And hurry!"

At that, Fuzzy scurried off, leaving the ceiling tile askew. Hopefully, his distraction would delay the principal long enough that she wouldn't run into Mr. Brittle and derail the pets' plans. Fuzzy couldn't linger if he wanted to help out with their big number.

was a chance that Mr. Darius might figure out how he'd escaped and take measures to keep Fuzzy locked up for good. But that was another problem for another day.

Hustling through the crawl space, Fuzzy reached the spot where the music room should be. Had he arrived in time? Moving as cautiously as a cat in a kennel of sleeping Rottweilers, he slid aside a ceiling tile and peeked through the gap.

The room was dark aside from a spotlight illuminating Mr. Brittle, who had apparently just stepped through the door.

Holding up a hand to shade his eyes, the teacher called, "Mrs. Flake?"

And ready or not, it was showtime.

CHAPTER 16

Cloudy with a Dance of Meatballs

"One-two-three-four,
We're singing 'bout the business that we all adore!"

The music room's stereo blasted the song, a hip-hop version of some old tune about show business. At the sound, Mr. Brittle grimaced and recoiled as if the music was physically painful. He whirled, reaching for the door. But Luther the boa had twined himself around the push bar, blocking his exit. (Luther preferred this to dancing.)

The sub shrieked like a kindergartner finding a dead spider in her Underoos.

"Mrs. Flake, this is not funny!" he cried.

The spotlight flipped, illuminating the empty riser where the choir normally stood. From out of the darkness, Cinnabun leaped in a mighty hop right onto the platform. With arms spread wide, she sashayed forward to the beat, waggling her "jazz paws."

Fuzzy didn't know whether her dancing was any good. But one thing was for certain: The bunny sure knew how to make an entrance.

And speaking of entrances, it was high time he made his. Fuzzy was supposed to appear on that makeshift stage in less than a minute, but here he sat, still peeking out of the ceiling far above.

First Mistletoe, then Sassafras showed up on the spotlit riser, flanking Cinnabun. The trio moonwalked with attitude to spare, singing along at top volume even though they knew the substitute couldn't understand them. Mr. Brittle had clapped his hands over his ears when the music first hit; now he gaped at the three pets as if he thought he might be losing his mind.

Fuzzy scanned the music room, seeking an easy way down. Nothing looked easy. No tall bookshelves or cabinets that a visitor from above could step down onto. How had the other pets made their way inside?

He spotted a long banner of purple fabric attached to the ceiling tile beside him with a square of silver duct tape. Its other end was anchored directly above the riser. In fact, now that he noticed it, the banner was one of nearly a dozen cloth strips in different hues shooting out from the hub like the spokes of a rainbow wheel.

The music swelled as it went into the chorus. Hopping onto the little stage, Marta and Igor joined the trio's wild dancing. (Actually, Igor hopped; Marta crawled.) Fuzzy should have been down there already. He noticed Marta squinting against the spotlight, searching for him.

It was now or never.

Every instinct told him not to do what he was thinking of doing. But he'd overcome his instincts before, at Mr. Brittle's apartment, and lived to tell about it.

Bracing himself, Fuzzy reached out and grabbed the end of the purple cloth. He tugged and felt the duct tape loosen. So far, so good. What he didn't know was whether the other end was anchored more securely. Fuzzy gritted his teeth.

One way to find out.

In a gut-wrenching move, he pushed off with his hind legs and dropped into space.

Shhhick went the tape as it released.

"Aaaahhhh!" screamed Fuzzy, not quite in the same key as the song.

The floor raced up to meet him at an alarming rate. Fuzzy squeezed his eyes shut. Was he about to become a guinea pig pancake?

When his full weight hit the fabric, it nearly yanked the cloth from his paws. Fuzzy clung on for dear life, and suddenly he was swinging, not falling. Opening

his eyes, he found himself speeding straight for the riser like a rodent Tarzan.

Dead ahead, Cinnabun and the other pets were traipsing across the platform in what she'd called a grapevine step (though Fuzzy didn't see what dancing had to do with grapes). One by one, each pet stopped to belt out a line of the song.

All this Fuzzy witnessed as he flew closer and closer.

Then, just before he reached the riser, one vitally important question popped into his mind:

How the heck do I stop?

The cloth strip answered the question for him. At the last second, it tore loose from the staples pinning it to the ceiling.

Suffering mange mites!

He was in free fall—and headed straight for Igor!

Sensing movement from the corner of his gaze, the iguana began to look up.

Whomp! Fuzzy barreled into him at warp speed.

Ba-boomf! Down they both went, like a sack of seed. But they weren't the only sacks of seed.

Because Igor slammed into Sassafras, who stumbled into Marta, who knocked over Mistletoe. Before you could say *shimmy-shuffle-sham*, the whole chorus line, except Cinnabun, lay sprawled on the stage in a massive tangle.

The next few seconds were a blur of limbs and tails, of fur and feathers and scales. When Fuzzy could focus, he found himself sitting on Igor's chest as the iguana flailed away at him, eyes squeezed shut.

"Gah!" cried Igor. "Help, space invaders! Flying monkeys!"

Fuzzy caught his feet. "Chill, Igor!"

"Oh, it's you." The iguana opened his eyes. "Might have known."

Meanwhile, the music thump-thumped along and Cinnabun kept right on dancing. Past her, Fuzzy could make out Mr. Brittle staring at the stage, his mouth gaping like a hippo at feeding time.

The bunny noticed that her fellow dancers had fallen. "Get up!" she hissed, not missing a step. "The show must . . ."

Mistletoe encouraged her. "Go on."

"Exactly," said Cinnabun, nodding at the sub. "We can't win him over if we don't dance. So *dance*, y'all!"

Galvanized by her words, Fuzzy and the rest scrambled to their feet. Awkwardly, they found the beat and followed Cinnabun's steps as best they could. To call them as smooth as the Bolshoi Ballet would have been a slight exaggeration. Fuzzy spun left when he should have gone right; Marta tromped all over Mistletoe's feet; and Igor accidentally thwacked Sassafras with his tail.

But they kept on dancing.

Despite the missed steps and sour notes, despite the staggers and squeaks, the pets gave it their all. By the time they reached the final chorus, Fuzzy was surprised to discover himself belting out the tune with the enthusiasm of a Broadway hoofer on opening night. And when they spread across the stage in a kick line, he actually teared up a little.

For Fuzzy and his friends to expose their true abilities to a human this way was a risky move. And the pets were taking this risk wholeheartedly, for the good of Fuzzy's students.

A lump the size of a cantaloupe formed in his throat. This, what they were doing, was the truest definition of a class pet's mission. Caring for the kids came before everything—before pride, before comfort, even before safety. And whatever the result of their performance, Fuzzy felt honored to be on that makeshift stage at that moment with his fellow pets, singing and dancing to help the kids he loved.

At last the big finish arrived. Fuzzy and the other pets hit their ultimate note, struck their final "jazz paws" pose, and sent out their musical plea to the Meanest Sub in the Universe.

They held their pose for a long moment as the final chord faded.

The silence stretched.

Squinting against the spotlight's glare, Fuzzy peered at the slender figure of Mr. Brittle. The man's hands had dropped from his ears and were now covering his mouth. Was that a good thing or a bad thing? Fuzzy didn't know.

With the tip of his tail, Luther stretched away from the door's push bar and flicked on the overhead light switch. All the animals stared at Mr. Brittle. Had their gamble paid off, or were they now in deeper trouble than they'd ever seen before?

The sub was staring right back at them as if he'd just seen Abe Lincoln, the Abominable Snowman, and a three-eyed alien dance the Hokey Pokey. His unblinking eyes were as round as exercise wheels, his body stiff as a Popsicle stick. Slowly, Mr. Brittle's hands dropped from his mouth.

But still he didn't speak.

"Well?" squeaked Fuzzy at last. "Say something."

The substitute's gaze roamed the room. "Mrs. Flake? I—uh, you—the pets . . ."

"This guy's a teacher?" muttered Igor. "He can barely talk."

Fuzzy shushed him.

"I don't know where you are," said Mr. Brittle, "but that . . . that was indescribable."

Cinnabun beamed. "Did y'all hear that? We're indescribable."

A half smile, rare as an albino alligator, tugged at a corner of the sub's lips. "Really, that has got to be the worst dancing I have ever seen in my life."

CHAPTER 17

A Whiter Shade of Fail

Fuzzy's jaw fell open. They were the *worst*? He glanced at the other pets' crestfallen faces. Mistletoe's lower lip trembled. Igor looked ready to bite someone.

A sour taste flooded Fuzzy's mouth. All that work, all that risk, and for what?

They had failed.

Instead of inspiring the substitute to return to music, they had totally turned him off. Fuzzy's gut gave a queasy twist, like when he'd gotten into Miss Wills's chocolate strudel. He felt helpless and hopeless.

How could this be?

The cruel sub would keep on terrorizing his kids, and there was nothing Fuzzy could do about it.

Mr. Brittle barked a laugh, still looking about for Mrs. Flake. "I mean, kudos to you for training all these pets to move, more or less together. Seriously, that is pretty amazing. But their choreography? Ouch!"

"I didn't think it was so bad," Cinnabun muttered, studying her feet. Fuzzy patted her shoulder. The others slumped, mired in defeat.

As he strolled around the riser checking out the pets, the former teen idol shook his head. "A grape-vine step? Much too complicated. Their moonwalk was ridiculous. And you should never combine jazz hands with hip-hop."

Luther slithered down from his post on the door and curled up beside a nearby chair. He looked like he was considering constricting somebody.

"I did like when the guinea pig swung down and knocked them all over, though," said the sub. "Hilarious!"

Fuzzy's ears grew warm. He avoided meeting the other pets' eyes.

Finishing his circuit of the platform, Mr. Brittle stopped at the door. "If you really wanted to make an impression, you should have hired a choreographer who knows his stuff. And I will not even mention the singing—or whatever that was they were doing."

Sassafras pouted. "This dude is tone-deaf. I've got a terrific voice."

Igor was so bummed out, he didn't even make a snarky comment.

"Mrs. Flake?" the substitute called again. When still no answer came, he smirked. "Not claiming credit for your mistakes, *hmm*?" Mr. Brittle lingered a moment or two, waiting for a reply. The smirk faded. In almost a whisper, he added, "I know how that feels."

Then, slowly and thoughtfully, he opened the door and out he went. Before it closed, Fuzzy thought he heard the man humming the tune the pets had just been singing. Probably it was only the building's pipes moaning.

Fuzzy sighed a heavy sigh. For a handful of heart-beats, nobody spoke.

Then Cinnabun sniffled. "Well, y'all, I reckon we should be getting back to our cages. Tomorrow is another day." But her smile looked wobbly.

Jogged out of their gloomy trance, the other pets finally stirred.

Fuzzy swallowed around the painful lump in his throat. "Th-thanks, everyone," he choked out. "We gave it our best shot. I appreciate all of you."

Igor punched his shoulder. "Enough schmaltz, fur face. Iguanas don't do mushy." But his lower lip was quivering.

Without any fanfare, they trudged away to return to their own rooms. And that, Fuzzy thought, was that.

After the week he'd had, Fuzzy was beyond relieved when Miss Wills came to pick him up for the weekend, and happy to return to her house for some pampering. He soaked up the snuggles and snacks while listening for clues about when she might return to class.

But he was destined for disappointment. On Saturday, when Miss Wills called a friend, he heard her mention that the case was such a big one, her jury duty might not end for at least another week.

Upon hearing that, Fuzzy couldn't relax anymore. He dreaded the coming week, and he fretted about Mr. Brittle's threat. Could the sub really replace Miss Wills and Fuzzy too? And if he did, what would happen to Fuzzy? Miss Wills might not want to keep him at her house all the time. Would he have to go back to the pet store, saying good-bye to all his kids *and* his teacher?

A lump formed in his throat. For a class pet, not having a class was a fate worse than death.

First thing Monday morning, Miss Wills dropped Fuzzy off at the classroom before heading out for another day of jury duty. "Be good," she told him. "This trial should be wrapped up soon."

Soon? Soon couldn't come soon enough for Fuzzy.

He hunched into a corner of his cage and wouldn't play with his ball or other toys. Instead, he rested his chin on his paws and waited for the unavoidable arrival of the Meanest Sub in the Universe. That man was harder to defeat than a vampire in a Kevlar vest.

Students dragged into class in ones and twos. Here came Spiky Diego, looking solemn, and Messy Mackenzie, wearing a deep frown above her breakfast-spattered T-shirt. But no Mr. Brittle.

A few minutes later, there was a flurry at the door. In burst a short, round woman with an arm-load of papers and an angelic smile that spread across her face.

"So sorry I wasn't here to greet you all," she told the students, "but I just found out I'd be subbing for this class. The name's Miss Capstone."

Natalia frowned. "Where's Mr. Brittle?"

Dumping her papers onto the desk with a flourish, the woman blew a stray lock of hair away from her face. "Him?" She chuckled. "You'll never believe it."

Fuzzy rose and took a few steps forward. The first rays of hope warmed his chest.

"Why, what happened?" asked Diego, sitting up straight for the first time in days.

Miss Capstone flapped a hand. "He quit teaching, just like that."

Fuzzy gasped. A ragged cheer went up from the students.

"But he was going to show us double-entry book-keeping," said Sofia.

"Not anymore," said the new sub. "Your principal told me he's going to be on some TV show about boy bands, can you believe that?" Her laughter was rich and warm, like a mug of hot cocoa.

Rocking back onto his heels, Fuzzy sat in stunned silence for a moment. Then . . .

Wheek-wheek-wheek! He began jumping up and down in delight.

"Look!" cried Diego. "Fuzzy's popcorning!"

"He didn't like that guy any more than we did," said Heavy-Handed Jake.

Miss Capstone held up a palm. "But I haven't even mentioned the funniest part."

"What's that?" asked Maya.

"When he talked to Mrs. Flake, Mr. Brittle offered to choreograph a dance number with all your class pets for the school's holiday show!" The substitute shook her head. "What a nut!"

The kids laughed, and Fuzzy thought he'd never heard a sweeter sound. He felt lighter than a birthday balloon.

He just might be able to last until Miss Wills's jury duty was done, after all.

"Now, how about a read-aloud to start the day off right?" asked Miss Capstone. "Here's one of my favorites: *The Phantom Tollbooth*."

The students settled in to listen. Fuzzy curled up in his igloo, letting the tale wash over him like a warm tropical breeze.

Last week had been a long, tiring ordeal, but now that it was finally over, he needed to rest up and recover. After all, if he was going to be a hip-hop dance star in the holiday show, Fuzzy needed all his strength.